The Haunting of
Baker Street

Narrelle M Harris

Published by Dangerous Charm in 2024

Dangerous Charm
507/225 Elizabeth Street
Melbourne, VIC, 3000
Australia
Print Book ISBN: 978-1-7636499-3-4
These stories first appeared 2021-2024 at Narrelle M Harris' Patreon at
https://www.patreon.com/NarrelleMHarris
All stories © 2021-2024 Narrelle M. Harris
Cover designed by Narrelle M. Harris

Introduction

In February 2021, Melbourne entered its third Covid-19 lockdown. It only lasted a week, but it was enough to get me writing a whole new series of Sherlock Holmes stories for my Patreon.

I didn't recognise it at the time, but now I think that being restricted to my apartment, unable to leave except for brief periods of exercise or essential grocery shopping, might have inspired a story of two ghosts trapped inside the shape of their old home, barely able to be seen or heard, but waiting for an opportunity to connect with the world at large once more.

Thus was born The Haunting of Baker Street, written as a series of 221b ficlets (stories of exactly 221 words, the last word of each beginning with the letter B). It began in sadness, with the passing of John Watson as an old man, and then his beloved Sherlock. It continued in hope as their spirits found one another and held hands and kissed in their afterlife.

And so they haunt the shape of their old lodgings as they overlap the walls of a new apartment, built on the remains of an old Georgian townhouse – and where people who knew or admired Sherlock Holmes and John Watson have been leaving tributes for over a hundred years.

Into this restricted world come Martie and Caitlyn: two women who love each other and think the idea of a haunted apartment exciting. Their love, daring and compassion stand ready to help two blithe spirits find new purpose, and new mysteries to solve.

I hope you enjoy their adventures, told in blocks of 221 words – and may the love, friendship and adventurous spirit of Holmes and Watson continue for another 135 years!

Narrelle M Harris

June 2024

The Haunting of Baker Street

Sherlock found John sitting on the bench of their Sussex cottage. No breath stirred John's grey moustache. The lines of 85 wonderful years were terribly still in his beloved face. Resting in peace.

Sherlock kissed John's forehead. He sat beside his darling, took John's hand and held it, kissed it.

'Thank you, John. Thank you, my darling. Thank you for our lives together.'

He held John's cold hand and watched the sun set.

A month later, with nobody to remind him to take his pills – perhaps Sherlock wasn't interested in remembering – Sherlock fell among his bees.

That evening, young Teddy Wiggins was bringing fond greetings from his father, Sherlock's brightest Irregular, and found him there.

The funeral was small; the obituaries lavish. People who the Great Detective and his biographer had once helped left little tokens at their old London address. *Goodbye. Thank you.*

Teddy stored keepsakes of the great men in a small despatch box: Sherlock's ebony-hilted magnifying glass; John's fountain pen, with which he'd written fictionalised versions of their lives; letters they had written to each other, tied in red ribbon.

Odd things sometimes happened in the Wiggins household. Unsettling, though not sinister. When 221b was repaired after the war, Teddy buried the box inside the new foundations.

Unsettling things continued to happen.

A new story waited to begin.

221b Baker Street was not as it had been. The world turned and left the dead behind. Friends and lovers became mourners, became dust. Lives became legends, truth forgotten.

The bones of Baker Street became brittle. Part of its roof collapsed under a German bomb in 1941. An attempt to create a small hotel failed when its walls cracked. The foundations sank unevenly. Yet plans to demolish it for apartments, offices, shops, all came to nothing. It remained cheap lodgings.

It began, frankly, to earn a reputation.

Lodgers came and went.

Mostly, they went.

The once-famous tenants, Sherlock Holmes and Dr John Watson, were more myth than memory now. Nevertheless, strangers came to gaze up at their bow window. Some left flowers by the door. Letters sealed in wax. Ribbons tied to the railings; a candle for remembrance; final thank-yous; new pleas for help beyond giving. Prayers left for departed saints. Even in the 21st Century.

On foggy nights, some said, light shone from the hollow windows, across which shadows moved. The scent of ink, tobacco, chemicals lingered in the mouldering rooms, in the stairwell, in the street. A violin sang, strains lifting to the lonely stars.

A spectral voice sometimes grumbled, 'So many mysteries to solve, John, beyond my reach!'

And another would reply, 'Patience, Sherlock. Someone will come. Believe.'

'As you can see, we retained the façade and some of the interior as a nod to the heritage people. Sadly, the structural damage to the whole 221 row meant 221b couldn't be fully restored.'

Irish-pale Caitlyn Ransome noted the little clutter of notes and gifts by the wall, under the blue plaque that signified that this was the former 19th century home of the Great Detective and his biographer.

Murphy, the estate agent, scooped up the letters, flowers and a small jar of honey by the door. 'People leave all sorts,' she laughed.

'And as long as we clear the offerings, we get a reduced rent?'

'Yes,' said Murphy, too curtly.

Martie Burgess, Caitlyn's Anglo-Australian girlfriend, went straight to the unnerving point. 'And a discount for ghosts?'

'Baker Street isn't haunted!' protested Murphy, alarmed. 'Who said it was haunted?'

'The neighbours,' grinned Martie. 'They say nobody stays more than a month.'

'And we know the last person who tried,' contributed Caitlyn. 'Jason reported chemical smells, tobacco smoke, a vanishing wood fire in the electric fireplace, violin music too, voices, and moving shadows in the sitting room.'

'Which is why the rent is so cheap,' said Martie.

Caitlyn took the letters from the gawping agent's hands. 'We'll take it,' she said. 'I like ghosts, and I never could resist a bargain.'

Caitlyn and Martie took possession of their new rental that week.

The fact that something else was "in possession" became clear as they attempted to shelve their books, which flung themselves onto the floor as soon as they turned. Hair prickled all over their scalps, but they refused to be spooked.

'We're staying,' snapped Caitlyn. 'Get used to it.'

Martie shelved a book. As they watched, it jerked free into open space and...

...hovered.

'Good,' murmured Martie. 'Showing *some* respect.'

She took the signed 1894 edition of *The Memoirs of Sherlock Holmes* from the air. It fell open to the inscription.

To Sherlock Holmes. Enjoy your new microscope too, courtesy of my poor scribblings. John H Watson. A counter-note read: *It is still romanticised.*

Martie placed it reverently in alongside a modern set of Watson's writings and a slim blue volume on queen bees. When nothing else happened, she said: 'Enough poltergeisting for one day?'

The air did not reply.

Holmes brooded before the apparition of a fire. He habitually ignored the building's new attic, visible through the ghost of the old sitting room.

'They have all my books!' Watson exclaimed, his delight offset by Holmes' pique.

'Hmph.'

'I like them.'

'Yes, well, they have your books.'

'They're brave. They have your book too.'

Holmes scoffed. 'They don't even keep bees.'

Caitlyn, an architect, had questions about the refurbished, very irregular 221b Baker Street.

The building was shorter than expected, each floor's ceiling lower than the high Georgian original. Planned extra storeys had not eventuated. Blueprints and materials had frequently vanished, along with memory of them, during construction. The current attic level, from whence ghostliness emanated, equated to the old second floor.

Walking home, arm in loving arm with Martie, Caitlyn spotted their incorporeal flatmates.

'Sneaky devils,' Caitlyn grinned. In the small attic window were indistinct shades of two men, kissing.

The profiles, like cameo portraits, were immediately identifiable: the slender build and hawklike nose of one, the broad shoulders and moustache of the other. Combined with the address, the deduction was obvious.

'They're still together,' said Martie happily.

Ghostly hand in hand, Sherlock and John kissed in their old room, a shadow overlaying the new attic, grateful for this almost insubstantial yet comforting touch.

They only impinged on the world with recalled sound and shade. Through force of will, they made the air rush and wrenched objects from places of rest.

What would John give to wield a pen again? What would Sherlock sacrifice to speak directly to the living?

Anything but each other. It's why their spirits lingered. They refused to be parted. Not even death could break their bond.

Understanding that their poltergeists were Sherlock Holmes and John Watson was simple, after Caitlyn and Martie saw their silhouettes against the attic window.

Understanding their motivations took a few more weeks.

One morning, the attic hatch obligingly fell open, enticing Martie to explore.

She plonked a dusty cardboard box on the table, beside the week's door-stoop offerings. (Most were sweet but dull, but Martie tried to reply to others.) Opening the box revealed it was full of equally dusty letters.

'Holmes' old unopened mail's stowed up there.'

Caitlyn poked at it. 'Might as well chuck 'em.'

Lifting the box, ever-inquisitive Martie meant only to move them for later reading.

An extremely localised whirlwind struck. Martie, alarmed, dropped the box, contents becoming a mini-tornado: paper, dust, desiccated moths.

Caitlyn was furious. 'Stop that at once! I don't care if you *are* Sherlock Bloody Holmes. We're *staying*.'

Everything collapsed instantly to the carpet.

'I don't think he's trying to scare us.'

Caitlyn's gaze followed Martie's to the single envelope resting at the centre of their table.

'He wants us to read his fan mail?'

The letter on the table rose of its own accord and stood impossibly on its edge.

Martie reached for it. The letter flew into her hand.

'All right, don't be so impatient,' she scolded the insistent ghost. 'Mr Bossy.'

The envelope in Martie's pale hand was unremarkable, apart from the fact it had flown to her on ghostly wings.

The contents were more interesting. Martie read aloud to her girlfriend and the loitering spirits of Holmes and Watson.

> *'Dear Mister Holmes,*
>
> *I know you can't really help me, but I have to tell someone, and nobody will listen.*

Someone is trying to drive me mad. I hear voices in the walls. Objects keep moving; or disappearing and showing up days later. I have blackouts, losing hours. Days, sometimes. I can always taste blood afterwards.

I'm not imagining it. The voices aren't just in my head, whatever my mother says. I'm not mad, but maybe I will be. I can't stand it anymore.

If only you were still around, I know you'd believe me. I know you'd help me. I'll hang on to my sanity as long as I can, because I know you'd want me to.

Yours, Meredith Winter.'

'Poor kid,' said Caitlyn. 'When's it dated?'

'Four months ago, from Archway, here in London. I wonder if she's still there.'

Caitlyn was already Googling. 'Found her. Her social media photos look haggard.'

The Baker Street ghosts swirled across the discarded letters on the carpet in approval.

Martie grinned. 'Let's text her and let Mr Holmes give her help From Beyond.'

Sherlock Holmes was thoroughly annoyed by his incorporeality. He had finally communicated usefully to the latest tenants, who'd vanished in pursuit of the promising mystery *without him*.

John Watson felt disembodiment wasn't a complete disaster. They could slightly influence the physical world; he could still hold Sherlock's hand and press a kiss to his cheek. Even if it were a mere feat of imagination, it was enough.

And what were they now but the persistent imaginings of their most intense emotions? Sherlock's burning curiosity and John's devotion to Sherlock, which had survived all manner of discouragement.

Sherlock reciprocated that love with fewer words but unmistakable fervour.

Their spirits had returned tied to the keepsakes Teddy Wiggins kept in John's old despatch box, never heard and rarely seen.

But then tiny Annie had taken John's pen to write a letter to her Poppa Billy. Small, ferocious whirlwinds had wracked the cottage until the pen, containing John's spirit, sat again alongside Sherlock's magnifying glass.

That despatch box now bound them to Baker Street. Sherlock theorised (on scant data) that its precious contents might eventually allow stronger manifestations. He speculated on the capacity for greater *form* and *presence*.

Actually, John thought that Sherlock, who delighted in the theatrical, simply longed to speak directly to living people, even if it was just to say BOO!

Caitlyn and Martie returned from Archway, despondent. The day after agreeing to meet, their "client" Meredith Winter had fallen; smashed her head; was in ICU in a coma.

'I don't like it,' Martie said, darkly. 'That timing is suspicious.'

A frame rattled on the mantelpiece, indicating ghostly agreement, or possibly exasperation.

Caitlyn slumped into an armchair. 'Maybe she really has some disorder. Aural hallucinations. Blackouts...'

Meredith's letter on the table flapped on a sudden ghostly breeze.

Martie agreed with Mr Holmes. 'It's a weird coincidence, the day we arranged to meet her.'

The living inhabitants of Baker Street, glum at a truncated adventure, went for dinner to restore their spirits. Their tipsy, giggling return resulted in Martie fumbling the keys. They dropped into the little-used Georgian area below.

Caitlyn, less drunk and more slender, climbed over the railing and down. She found the keys gleaming in the darkness, but before attempting the upward climb, she paused.

'Martie?'

'Yeah, baby?'

'There's something down here.'

'Is there, Pum'kin?'

'Some of Mr Holmes' mail. Arranged.' Caitlyn couldn't help giggling again. 'Arranged suspiciously like an arrow.'

Martie tried to climb the railing but fell back onto the street. She swore, ripely Aussie.

'Martie-babe, the mortar's crumbling.'

There followed the odd sound of metal on stone, then Caitlyn said: 'There's something behind this loose brick.'

Martie and Caitlyn, intrigued and excited, had placed a small steel box on their dining table. Martie fetched a screwdriver to jimmy it open.

The ghost of Sherlock Holmes watched avidly. The ghost of John Watson was less thrilled, his gaze shifting between the box, recovered from 221 Baker Street's foundations, and Sherlock, who was wan, even for a ghost.

'Why did you expend so much of your energy signposting its location?'

'You cannot tell?'

'No. And it's dangerous. You know what's in it!'

'The mementos that Wiggins kept after our passing.'

'Our letters, Sherlock!' John's distress was evident.

'We are beyond the censure of an unforgiving law, my dear,' said Sherlock gently. He took John's hand in his, and immediately his ethereal presence strengthened. 'Allow me to explain.'

John calmed, trusting in Sherlock's motives, as always.

'I know you, too, have noticed that we are more... present, in the space where our private rooms once were.'

'And here, our former parlour, where so many adventures began.'

'Exactly. Letters addressed to us further consolidate us. I theorise that the contents of this box may permit increased manifestation.'

Martie whooped in triumph and even Sherlock displayed apprehension as the women examined the contents.

A bundle of handwritten letters; a fountain pen; a magnifying glass; and a key to a safe deposit box.

When little Annie Wiggins borrowed the old fountain pen to write to grandpa, John Watson's spirit was so alarmed he created whirlwinds that tangled Annie's hair, blew paper across the room, blasted petals from their flowers, and made Annie cry.

John was ashamed of scaring her, afterwards, but he'd been terrified at that sudden separation of his pen and Sherlock's magnifying glass.

Now, as Caitlyn and Martie studied the contents of the box, Watson's ghost was strangely quiescent.

Caitlyn read the faded writing on the tag attached to the key: Snell & Passmore, Lawyers. 'I wonder if they're still around.'

'Google will know,' said Martie. And then she touched the narrow ribbon tied around the letters.

A tiny, fierce whirlwind broke out, snatching the letters up and away.

But the ribbon was old and frail. It broke. The letters scattered then rose, spinning in furious eddies.

In the middle of the swirling papers was an indistinct figure. A man, tall and broad-shouldered; face unclear.

The women should have been afraid, but while unexpected, the whirlwind didn't feel *dangerous*.

Now, another ghost appeared: taller, thinner. It seemed to hold the other's hand, and the whirlwind ceased. Letters fell. The figures remained, side by side.

One letter had fallen open to reveal the first line.

Dearest Sherlock, my love.

And the last.

Beloved.

The incriminating letter lay open as a heart among all those scattered on the carpet.

Two indistinct ghosts held misty hands. Of similar heights, the broad-shouldered one held itself with military correctness yet communicated great distress. The elegantly tall one lifted a defiant chin.

Martie bent her knees and carefully closed the letter and, rising, held it towards them.

'Don't be afraid,' she said gently, with some irony.

John Watson's spirit reached for the letter. As his hazy hand touched the ancient paper, he became more visible: his handsome, moustached face; his stricken expression, the fine shape of his trembling hands.

His voice, not truly heard by the living in a hundred years, filled the room.

Burn them, he pleaded.

Martie gasped; Caitlyn answered.

'It's okay. Love like ours, that's allowed now.'

John's anxiety didn't abate. The blur beside him spoke.

*Observe, John. Two women who love as we did. As we **do**. The world has changed.*

*They're **private**, Sherlock.*

'We won't read them,' promised Martie, even though she was dying to; but she had more compassion and better manners than that.

'I'll wrap them all in new ribbon and put them in the attic,' promised Caitlyn.

Please. Sherlock's spirit leaned against his ghostly love. *I treasure them.*

Then Sherlock, too, become more... *present*: thin face, piercing eyes, hawk-like nose. Beautiful.

Martie reverently folded the love letters, unread, into a stack. Caitlyn presented her with a thin white ribbon, formerly used to hold a roll of blueprints. Holmes and Watson had faded, but a faint smear in the air showed that they lingered.

The women, tipsy on their return home, had sobered up since opening the box for their resident ghosts. Now, while Martie made a pretty bow, Caitlyn reflected on the unhappy result of their attempted investigation of the Archway Mystery.

'What can we do about Meredith Winter?' she asked the air.

The smear in the air swirled. Were they all manifested out? With a sigh, Caitlyn ran her fingers over the magnifying glass still nestled in the box. She picked it up and, on a whim, peered through it at the ghostly smudge.

Only to squeak with sudden fright and almost drop the glass.

Martie started in sympathy. 'What?!'

The smudge intensified. Caitlyn held the glass out to her girlfriend. 'Try it. Don't drop it. If it breaks I don't know what'll happen.'

Cautiously, Martie took the glass and peered through it.

Beyond it, looking as solid and real as though they lived and breathed, were, unmistakably the sleuths of Baker Street.

Sherlock, elated, grinned. 'Just as I told you!'

Watson, obviously reassured, gestured towards the fountain pen; practically beckoned.

Martie gave the magnifying glass to Caitlyn and, encouraged by John Watson's gesturing ghost, took up the fountain pen.

'How's he looking?' Martie asked.

'I'm right here, young lady,' said a warm, astonished voice.

A more solid-looking Watson seemed almost as surprised as she felt, to be heard so clearly; to be standing beside the equally almost-corporeal presence of Sherlock Holmes.

The two men looked as solid as the furniture, but as Watson approached Martie, he walked through a chair then halted halfway through the dining table. He was suddenly all embarrassed confusion. 'Oh. Oh dear.'

'No probs,' said Martie, not knowing where to look.

'I was hoping to retrieve my pen.'

She offered it to him, aware of Caitlyn and Sherlock Holmes watching keenly. Watson's hand passed right through the pen; through Martie's hand as well. She jumped as though jolted with electricity.

Watson's ears went pink; he retreated rapidly. 'My dear young lady, a thousand apologies.'

Martie hand tingled. 'That's okay. It didn't hurt. Just feels funny.'

'It was an unwarrantable intrusion on my part.'

'No worries, really,' she said, growing more Australian by the second. 'It's not like we've got a Madame Spookorama's Guide to Ghostly Etiquette on hand.'

'Quite,' responded Holmes, amused. 'Though perhaps "do not inhabit the space occupied by the living" is a good beginning.'

They made a peculiar quartet around the table: Martie in one chair, her grip on the fountain pen lending its long-dead owner a more intense presence. Caitlyn sat adjacent, holding the magnifying glass that likewise made Sherlock Holmes more corporeal.

Holmes and Watson stood across from them, translucent. Holmes looked very pleased with himself.

'You see, John, how my surmise was correct! Human interaction with the last artefacts of our lives enables us to manifest clearly. And now!' he clapped his hands together, the sound distinct and sharp, and turned avidly to the women.

'Miss Ransome. Miss Burgess. Tell me more about Meredith Winter. Your report to date has been woeful. Even John was more observant in his time.'

This remark pleased nobody; not even John. Holmes shrugged. 'If I could see our client personally, I may make more progress!'

'Unfortunately, we can't leave Baker Street, so we'll have to make do,' said Watson briskly.

'Of course we can leave Baker Street,' asserted Holmes. 'We didn't start here.'

'You didn't?' Caitlyn asked, surprised.

'No,' agreed John slowly. 'I manifested first at our Sussex cottage.'

'Keeping me company to the last,' replied Sherlock fondly. 'Then I died and I joined you there, until Wiggins finalised our affairs and brought the despatch box to London.'

'And thence here,' said John, 'where we belong.'

Martie felt self-conscious to be carrying John Watson's pen – and therefore his ghost – in her pocket. He remained politely quiet, beyond a soft 'Oh!' as she and Caitlyn left Baker Street.

Sherlock's magnifying glass was in Caitlyn's handbag, which she wore across her body, anxious that today of all days, some thief would try to snatch it. Holmes' spirit was either silent or inaudible, all the way on the Tube to Archway.

At Whittington Hospital, the women confidently asserted their close friendship with the patient; a harried nurse allowed them entry.

Meredith Winter was in the public ward, a curtain pulled around her bed, unconscious and without visitors. A bruise bloomed on her forehead and into her hairline, mottling her brown skin.

The pen in Martie's pocket pulled disconcertingly towards the end of the bed.

'Chill, Doc,' muttered Martie, withdrawing the pen. It guided her to the dangling medical chart. A moment later, Dr Watson materialised, bending over the notes. 'Chemicals were found in her blood, Sherlock.'

Caitlyn's handbag shook and, cautiously, she reached in for the glass. Once in her hand, it pulled her towards the woman in the bed. Holmes manifested faintly and, peering at her, said:

'Miss Winter. We've come to solve your case.'

Suddenly, the spirit of Meredith Winter sat bolt upright within her supine physical body.

The incorporeal Meredith Winter gazed at the strangers in her room.

'You look like Sherlock Holmes,' she said, dubiously.

'I *am* Sherlock Holmes,' said Sherlock impatiently. 'This is Dr Watson. You wrote to us.'

Meredith gasped. 'But you're dead. Does... that mean I'm dead too?'

'No,' said John, his bedside manner gentle. 'Your body is unconscious, due to a head wound. Your brave *soul* is speaking with... we unquiet spirits.'

Martie showed her John's pen. 'Caity and I gave them a lift.'

Caitlyn waggled the magnifying glass in greeting. Both pretended they weren't now speaking with the not-quite-dead.

Meredith glanced through her transparent hand at her flesh-and-blood one on the sheets. '*Can* you help me?'

'You had unusual chemicals in your bloodstream, Miss Winter. Aminobutyric acid. Chlorophenyl,' Sherlock enunciated carefully from her chart.

'But I don't take anything!'

'That doesn't mean you have not ingested anything,' said John, ominously. 'Your letter said you had blackouts and tasted blood. Not uncommon side effects.'

'And hearing voices?'

'Associated with some disorders,' said Sherlock. 'Narcolepsy. Brain lesions.'

John flashed him a sharp look and said, 'I see no indication of that.'

Caitlyn suddenly stumbled to the bed, pulled by the magnifying glass. She held it beside Meredith's pale face and Sherlock peered closely.

'Watson, look,' he said. 'What do you deduce about this bruise?'

Watson's ghost examined Meredith's scalp. 'What happened, Miss Winter?' he asked.

'My mother called me down for tea. I remember going to the top of the stairs but I must have blacked out and fallen down them.'

John studied her skull and what he could see of her unblemished arms and body. 'This isn't right, Holmes.'

'You see it!' Holmes was tactlessly triumphant.

'It's an odd shape,' said John. 'The edges of steps or banisters would leave multiple contusions. This mark is more consistent with a single blow.'

'Exactly! This is suggestive; combined with the chemicals, almost certain, although the culprit is unclear. Tell me, Miss Winter, is anyone in your household on strong prescribed medications?'

'My brother's girlfriend was on anti-spasmodics after she injured her back skiing. Mum nursed Lizzie through her recovery.' Her hurt showed.

'She hasn't nursed you?' Martie asked.

'No,' said Holmes firmly. 'Her letter clearly states that her mother didn't believe her. Does she know you wrote for help?'

'She posted my letter.'

Holmes gestured towards Caitlyn's pocket. Caitlyn promptly withdrew her phone to search for anti-spasmodics and their side effects. Holmes read the screen results eagerly.

'I fear, Miss Winter,' he said gently, 'you have been subjected to medical maltreatment and assault in your home. Your symptoms are consistent with the side effects of Baclofen.'

'I'm not familiar with this treatment,' confessed Watson. 'Does your tiny library describe it further?'

Caitlyn studied the website. 'It's an odourless crystalline powder, off-white and water-soluble.'

Meredith was baffled. 'But I haven't taken any pills. How did...?'

'Through your food or drink,' said Holmes.

'Strong coffee could mask any flavour,' said Caitlyn.

'Or you could hide it in cake icing,' suggested Martie. 'That's how we used to give tablets to our Labrador.'

Three ghosts gave her a *Look*.

'The better question is, who administered it?' said Holmes firmly. 'Doubtless, the same person who struck you on the stairs. The culprit is obvious, even Watson knows.'

'Your mother,' said John gently.

'No!' But Meredith's frightened eyes said 'yes'.

The door flew suddenly open; Martie, startled, dropped the pen.

'Who are you people?' the woman demanded, giving them a sharp, suspicious glare.

Caitlyn hid the magnifying glass by shoving it under the blanket. The ghosts had all vanished. 'Friends. We came to see how Meredith's doing.'

'Well, she needs her rest. Off you pop,' she insisted. Mrs Winter bustled them furiously outside then closed the door, before turning to pat her daughter's hand.

'There, there, Merry,' she said. 'Mum's here. I wish you hadn't made me hit you, but now there's no need for more of that nasty medicine. Isn't that better?'

Meredith's spirit, trapped between grief and anger, gawped at her mother. 'Mum! Why are you doing this to me?'

Mrs Winter, patting her unconscious daughter's hand, didn't reply.

The men Meredith had asked for help manifested. Dr Watson's shade stood protectively by her bandaged head. Holmes' studied Meredith's oblivious mother.

'I don't understand why she's done this,' Meredith told them. 'We weren't close, but I didn't think she hated me.'

'I think... it's more complicated than that,' said Watson gently.

'She hated how close I was to Grandpop. She was jealous, I think. But he died months ago.'

Holmes responded with sharp interest. 'What of his estate?'

'I suppose Mum got everything.'

'It's all Dad's fault,' said Mrs Winter suddenly, perhaps influenced by the unheard, ghostly conversation. 'Passing me over in his will. That's not right. I don't have to hide the letters anymore, at least, and I'll manage everything as your guardian. What a relief. It would have been too awful to have to take advantage of being your next of kin.'

Meredith's hand twitched. Her eyes opened. 'Next of kin?' she cried as she tried to sit up.

'Oh, Merry, no! Lie down! Stop it!'

'No!'

Mrs Winter panicked. She snatched at a pillow; pushed it over Meredith's face.

But then a sudden, ferocious, freezing wind began to blow.

The tempest drove the shrieking Mrs Winter into the corner, as far from Meredith as possible. Meredith staggered out of bed and clung to the mattress to stay notionally upright. 'How could you?!' she cried out, in rage, fear, hurt, over the tumult. 'You tried to *kill* me!'

'No! I wouldn't!' But Mrs Winter's questionable denial was belied by how she clung to the pillow she'd meant to use for the attempt.

The door flew open, an alarmed duty nurse leading the charge, with Martie and Caitlyn on her heels. Wind whipped their hair as though they stood in a gale.

'*You tried to suffocate me*!'

'*You were supposed to stay asleep*!' The confession bellowed into sudden, still silence.

The nurse called for security. Caitlyn ran to Meredith. Martie stood menacingly between them and Mrs Winter. She felt rather than saw Doctor Watson beside her, his rage barely contained.

Mrs Winter, realising what she held, flung the pillow away. It flew up from the floor and back into her arms just as the guard arrived.

Mrs Winter, whimpering, tried to drop it; it wouldn't fall.

'You're *guilty*,' Holmes muttered in her ear. She wept, defeated, as did Meredith.

'I'm calling the police,' said the nurse. 'And you, unquiet spirit,' she added, matter-of-factly, 'she's given up; her daughter's safe. Let her be.'

They left Meredith in the care of her brother and returned home. Martie collected the latest letters from the doorstep and returned the magnifying glass and pen to their box while Caitlyn made tea. The ghosts lingered, Holmes exuding a sense of accomplishment while Watson radiated indignation.

'What an awful woman,' said Martie unhappily.

'She was the girl's *mother*,' protested Watson.

'How many fathers have we met who failed to protect their daughters?' Holmes challenged.

'Too many,' acknowledged Watson.

Caitlyn insisted on seeing the positives. 'We saved Meredith.'

Martie perked up. 'We did. And we can help others!' Martie tore open an envelope and laughed. 'Dear Sherlock Holmes,' she read, 'I know you're only fictional...'

Holmes glowered.

'If you ghosts are still here, you must have unfinished work,' Martie declared.

'Perhaps,' allowed Holmes.

'And people believe in you enough to write,' said Caitlyn.

'And you're real enough to help,' said Martie.

'And now we have agents to intervene in the living world on our behalf,' said Watson. 'Don't we?'

'Well, it *is* part of our rental agreement,' agreed Martie.

Holmes raised his head, buoyed by the growing eagerness. Watson brushed the back of his hand with his own; smiled warmly at Holmes, and then at Martie and Caitlyn.

'It appears,' he said, 'that our Baker Street consultancy is back in business.'

Acknowledgements

Thanks must, as always, go to Arthur Conan Doyle, for his creation of Sherlock Holmes and his perfect foil, Dr John Watson. I came for the adventures, I stayed for the friendship, and I've been here for nearly thirty years!

I always want to thank KCS, aka kcscribbler, who in 2008 invented the 221b ficlet challenge to write a ficlet of exactly 221 words, the last word of which must start with the later 'B' – and invited their fellow fans on fanfiction.net to join in!

A big shout-out to my glorious Patreon supporters, who help me to write more:

Adelle; D C Sams; Sarah Remy; Julia Hilton; Kim Fasching; Tim Richards; Kimber; Beck; Carey Handfield; sbbeasley; Adam Salisbury; Alice Harris; Lora Timonin; Melinda McCormack; Milane Duncan-Frantz; Sally; Champagne and Socks; Grant Watson; Jack Fennell; Richard Koehler; Sarah Drosendahl; Tansy Rayner Roberts; and Mike Thompson.

Big hugs and kisses to my personal support team too:

Chuck McKenzie who kindly gave of his time to talk me through the self-publishing process!

Tim Richards for always looking out for me.

Atlin Merrick for all the many ways in which she is my sister and kindred spirit, as well as her keen edits, suggestions on the cover, and her always valued and essential support.

And you, dear reader. Thanks for picking up this little series of 221b ficlet that make up a ghost story about an enduring friendship that has lasted for over 137 years!

With gratitude,
Narrelle M. Harris

Read on for more books (and extracts) by Narrelle M Harris

The Adventure of the Colonial Boy *and* The Swordmaster's Secret and Other Stories

The Adventure of the Colonial Boy

1893. Dr Watson, still in mourning for the death of his great friend Sherlock Holmes, is now triply bereaved, with his wife Mary's death in childbirth.

Then a telegram from Melbourne, Australia intrudes into his grief. 'Come at once if convenient.' Both suspicious and desperate to believe that Holmes may not, after all, be dead, Watson goes as immediately as the sea voyage will allow.

Soon Holmes and Watson are together again, on an adventure through Bohemian Melbourne and rural Victoria, following a series of murders linked by a repulsive red leech and one of Moriarty's lieutenants. But things are not as they were. Too many words lie unsaid between the Great Detective and his biographer. Too much that they feel is a secret.

Solve the crime, forgive a friend, rediscover trust and admit to love. Surely that is not beyond that legendary duo, Sherlock Holmes and Dr John Watson in Narrelle M Harris[1] *The Adventure of the Colonial Boy*.

Praise for *The Adventure of the Colonial Boy*

'Melancholy, sweet, triumphant, fierce in a beautiful balance.' ~ TA Creech, Amazon

'I found the second reading as exciting as the first.' ~ Heras Mom, Amazon

---

1. https://improbablepress.com/pages/narrelle-m-harris

'Harris' love of the detective and his doctor shine in every line; these men are in good hands with Narrelle as their biographer!' ~ Atlin Merrick

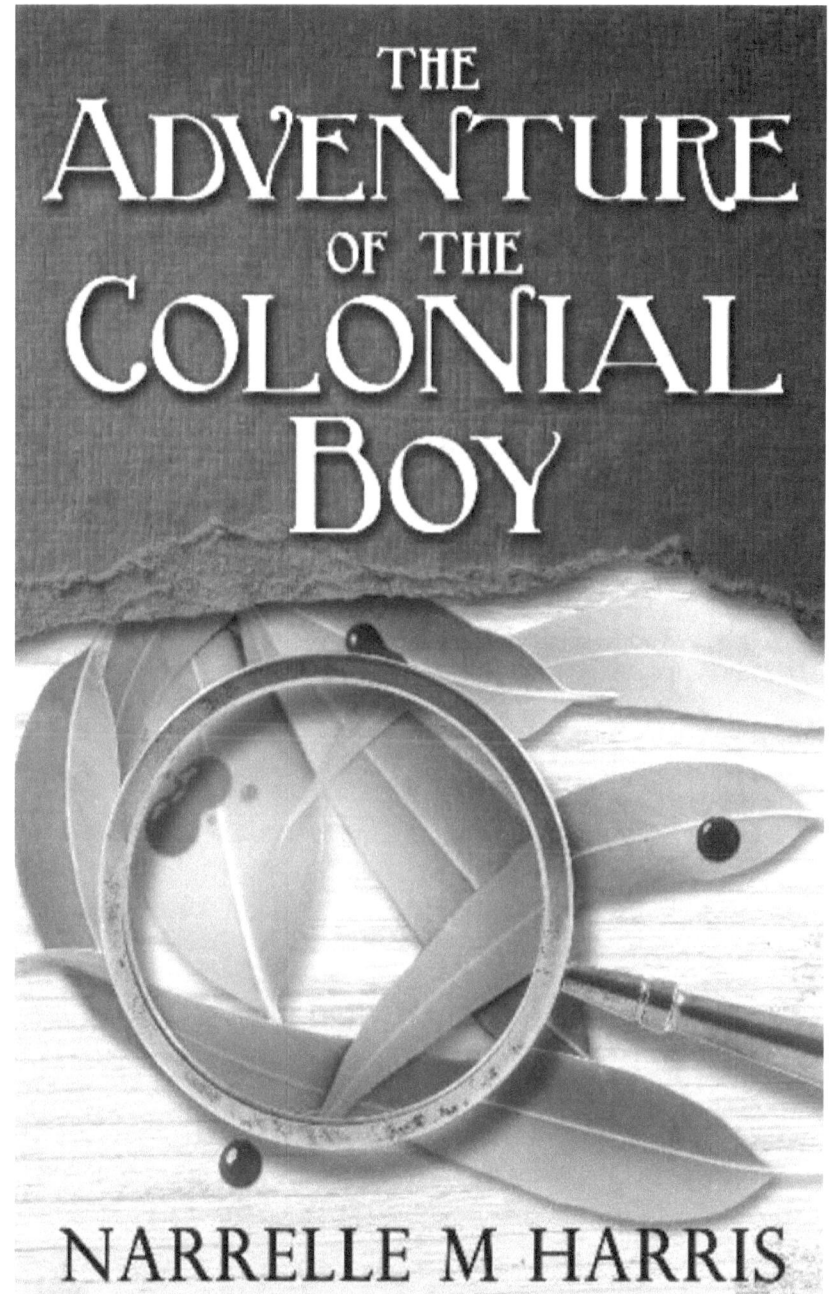

THE
ADVENTURE
OF THE
COLONIAL
BOY

NARRELLE M HARRIS

The Swordmaster's Secret and Other Stories

These stories are all set after the events of Narrelle M Harris' *The Adventure of the Colonial Boy*. The collection begins with "The Swordmaster's Secret", a few months after Sherlock Holmes and Dr John Watson return to London in 1894.

The stories follow Sherlock and John's lives together down the years, solving mysteries, and including a meeting with Oscar Wilde, a special Christmas, a case involving vinegar Valentines and a tale set in their retirement years in Sussex.

The book contains:

- ◈ The Swordmaster's Secret
- ◈ A Less than Ideal Gentleman
- ◈ God Rest ye Merry, Gentlemen;
- ◈ The Case of the Vinegar Valentine
- ◈ Winter Ice
- ◈ Bored
- ◈ The Beekeepers' Children.

The Swordmaster's Secret

and other stories

The Further Adventures of the Colonial Boy

NARRELLE M. HARRIS

Read on to sample the first three chapters of
The Adventure of the Colonial Boy

Extract from *The Adventure of the Colonial Boy*

Chapter One

Doctor John Watson found no relief from grief when he placed the final manuscripts for The Strand Magazine into an envelope. No; this memorial in text to his dead friend rendered the wound raw again, as though he was the one who'd done the murder at Reichenbach Falls, rather than that villain Moriarty. To write that sorry tale had made it true, dashing the last of Watson's denial.

Sherlock Holmes was dead, murdered by his great enemy and failed by his great friend.

Watson sealed the envelope, contemplating its contents gravely. For all the things he'd altered in his stories – to protect the innocent, to make a better tale, to obscure truths he was hardly able to articulate – one incident had been utterly unfabricated.

On learning Moriarty had escaped their net, Holmes had urged Watson to return to England, saying, 'You'll find me a dangerous companion now.' Watson's reply had been unequivocal. 'I will not go, Holmes. Nothing you say will induce me to leave your side in this business.'

Except that Holmes had induced him away, after all. He'd done it slyly, casually. The memory of it filled Watson with a hot flash of anger, and afterwards with guilt.

I'm angry with myself, not Holmes.

Watson didn't doubt Holmes had done it with the best of intentions; but Watson had returned to their Swiss boarding house at Holmes's greatest hour of need. For that, he could not forgive himself. After all those years working together, of their close friendship, he should have divined that the message about the sick Englishwoman was false.

Holmes's deliberate choice to let Watson leave did not, to Watson's mind, lessen his failure to stay by Holmes's side: not with the consequences that his failure entailed.

Well, the final story was written now. The Strand Magazine would publish Watson's remaining tales, however fancifully embellished. Each sprang from a true event and it would be for the public to read, judging both Holmes's genius and Watson's own fault in the matter.

Watson checked his pocket watch; it was not yet midday. A walk would do him good after so many days cloistered in his rooms, writing and rewriting.

He rose and pulled his dark coat over his black suit. He smoothed the black ribbon around the crown of his hat, put it on, then the black gloves.

Envelope tucked under one arm, he took his walking stick in hand and set out to deliver the manuscripts to The Strand's offices in Burleigh Street.

Afterwards, he would visit the cemetery and tell Mary that, for good or ill, the work was done at last.

The walk to South Kensington Station was pleasant on this clear September day. Watson stood on the platform, awaiting the train to Embankment, and watched its counterpart draw in on the other platform: the train to Baker Street. Watson's mouth pursed as the train departed, tugging him in the direction of those old rooms: of happier memories and the life he missed.

A sudden crowd of people jostled the doctor towards the platform's edge as his train drew in. Watson clutched tight to his manuscripts – he'd be damned if he lost the things by spilling them on the tracks – and braced against the unruly bustling. Someone behind him cursed, another man growled a response, and a hard shove shot Watson towards the lip of the platform. Only by jamming the tip of his cane into the ground was he saved from being propelled in front of the groaning, steaming bulk of the engine.

Watson turned angrily but the thoughtless instigators of his near miss had vanished. Scowling, he entered the train car and braced against the jerk and sway as it rolled into motion.

Alighting at Embankment he made his way up into the fresh air, strolling through the Victoria Gardens alongside the Thames, down the lane behind the Savoy, then up the short flight of stairs to The Strand.

There, he paused, arrested by memories prompted by those familiar buildings; the clop of hooves and rattle of carriages; the voices of men hailing one another or a hansom; the dust and smell of it, with the blue sky overhead, all the bustle and life of the London metropolis caught in microcosm.

This had been their London. The London of Holmes and Watson. How often had their adventures brought them here? What strange tales and astonishing mysteries had led them like hounds through these streets and alleys, into dingy boarding houses and smoky dens, or into handsomely furnished offices, grand halls, homes with a history of great or faded fortunes?

All of those wondrous exploits and their dazzling conclusions were at an end now. London was less than she had been, diminished by the loss of Sherlock Holmes, as was Watson.

The stories he'd written in a near frenzy over the last few years washed colour over the whole once more, painting every part of the city with the memory of the great detective. But nothing could truly capture the sound of Holmes's voice ringing out with thrilling purpose, the rich delight of his laughter, or the way they had laughed at absurdities. No words on paper could truly describe the bright gleam in Holmes's eye as he latched onto the clue that spelled doom for some malefactor; or the warm flush of Holmes's cheeks as his lassitude was galvanised into decisive activity. Nor the elegance of Holmes's hands, his gait, his whole person, whether engaged in a case or playing his violin to soothe Watson's fractured nerves...

Distracted by melancholy, Watson began to cross the great thoroughfare for Burleigh Street when a shout warned him of a carriage bearing down on him. Clutching the envelope and stepping aside, he found the horse had altered course and still bore down on him.

The driver had his fist tight-wrapped around the whip, which he brought down hard. The beast, eyes rolling against its hard use, lurched faster and would have run him down, except that a hand on Watson's collar jerked him back onto the footpath.

'Doctor Watson!' cried his rescuer, 'Watch your step! That growler almost had you, and then what would our old friend Mr Holmes have said to me, hmm? He wouldn't have been happy, I'll tell you that for free.'

Watson, frowning after the disappearing carriage, turned at the familiar voice. 'Why, Wiggins, is that you? I hardly recognise you!'

'To the life,' beamed Wiggins. He was much changed from the grubby street urchin who had been such an important part of life at Baker Street. He was a young man now, with the side-whiskers to prove it.

'Didn't Holmes find work for you as a messenger for The Graphic?'

'He did, and made sure I learned my letters and all. The editor liked my way with words, he said, and my colourful observations upon the life and denizens of the lower-down byways of London. He's training me up to be a reporter, now.'

Watson peered at the young man's hands and clothes. 'And you begin by drawing sketches of those denizens, I see.'

Wiggins laughed. 'You see the sketchbook in one coat pocket and my pencils in the other, Doctor Watson!'

'And the smudges upon your wrist, hand and fingers,' agreed Watson, 'The deduction was, as our friend would have said, elementary.'

'He'd no doubt have told you a dozen more things besides,' said Wiggins.

'Indeed, he would.'

'Such as I'm stepping out with Gill the Baker's daughter, Jane, who's a peach, though her father don't approve of me.' Wiggins's merry countenance sobered at last, his gaze flickering between the black band on Watson's hat and his black cotton gloves. 'I heard about your missus, Doctor Watson. I was very sorry for it, too. Mrs Watson was always very kind to me and the boys, if she happened on us, and she made that dolly for Georgie's sister Lottie when she was sick and we came to you.'

'Mary was a good soul,' said Watson, then ceased to speak, for what else could he say?

Wiggins recognised that here was a well of loss much too deep for easy conversation.

'Well, Doctor, I must be off to finish my drawings for Mr Rowley. You looked to be in a hurry yourself, taking more of your splendid stories to The Strand Magazine, I've no doubt. It's been grand to read them, and remember the great things Mr Holmes did. Even if I detect a little of what Mr Rowley calls artistic licence in them from time to time. Storytelling isn't courtroom testimony, is it Doctor Watson? No more than news is, says my editor.'

'No doubt your editor is right. Holmes was fond of The Graphic for its personal advertisements and a gossip column that assisted on more than one occasion.'

'I'll tell Mr Rowley so. He'll be right proud, what with your stories making Mr Holmes such a popular man about the country these days. Well, I hope to see you again, Doctor.'

'And I, you,' said Watson, 'And thank you for your timely intervention. Today has been a day for rowdy travellers, I'm afraid.'

Wiggins raised a hand in farewell and then was off, whistling, to find some local life to sketch for his paper. Watson gripped his walking stick and, with no further incidents, took his parcel of stories to the magazine's offices.

Some twenty minutes later, Watson was again out in the London early autumn, having irritably declined tea with his editor after their final exchange.

'Are you sure you won't reconsider, Doctor Watson? Holmes's exploits are so very popular with the reading public; I could publish them weekly for years to come.'

'Would that I could oblige you,' Watson had replied, jaw aching from gritting his teeth, 'But as Holmes died in Switzerland two and a half years ago, as I told you, I'm afraid there is no more suitable material for me to draw upon.'

'Surely you could invent...?' began the editor, then fell silent, no doubt quelled by the spark of rage he'd ignited in Watson's countenance. 'No, of course not. I see that. It's only that he is such a great loss to the field of criminology. To London, too. Our readers do quite feel that they know him, you know.'

'I'm pleased to hear it,' said Watson. That had been in part his intention: that the world should truly know his friend and understand the great loss he and they had suffered with his passing, 'But the fact remains there is nothing more to tell. He died defending them from a cruel and subtle mastermind of crime, and they should know it.'

'Indeed.' The editor had smiled. 'He was a hero, after Thomas Carlyle's notions, or so you write him.'

'And so he was,' said Watson stiffly, offended, 'At least to the degree that any flawed yet gifted human being may choose to behave as one.'

'I've no doubt of it,' the editor replied, backpedalling from any insinuation of exaggeration.

Watson had said his farewells and left in a simmering temper.

Certainly the stories were exaggerated in parts, but never Holmes's brilliance in solving the crimes. If sometimes he shone more light on Holmes's genius than his own contribution, what of that? Demonstrating Holmes's singular mind and great achievements had been the point of the stories. Where Watson had known things that Holmes had already understood, and it made better narrative sense to delay the reveal, why of course that's what he'd done. As in his telling of the tragic affair he'd written up as the Boscombe Valley case: Watson had known the Ballarat connection from the start, having spent formative years in the colony of Victoria. He'd in no way exaggerated Holmes's prowess; only written the tale to display it to best advantage.

And Holmes had certainly not been perfect. His surliness during Watson's courtship and marriage was a case in point, although he seemed to think well enough of Mary. Given time, he'd even deigned to visit them occasionally. But Holmes had let it be known since the moment she'd crossed their threshold – and Watson had dared to indicate that he thought her lovely – that love and marriage were the grossest sentimental claptrap and utterly anathema to him. He'd been downright waspish on the subject, which had merely served to convince Watson that he was correct to pursue Mary. Clearly there was no further profit in hoping...even had the strictures of society not prevented...

Watson's mind shied from completing either thought. Instead, he walked briskly, preferring the distracting bustle and energy of the task over a hansom or the Underground. He was alone with his thoughts too much already. A walk provided plenty of London's daily hubbub to keep his mind far from such dangerous and futile avenues.

At the cemetery, Watson bought a posy of violets from a dishevelled little girl at the gate. A grander bunch of flowers might be more appropriate, but Mary had always bought posies from the women and girls near their home, delighting in the simple blooms of violets, bluebells or heliotropes – and in the simple help such purchases offered to the poorer women of their town. So Watson bought flowers from little street urchins because Mary would have liked that.

At Mary's plot, he knelt to clear away the last visit's flowers and place the new posy in its decorative pot. A simple wooden marker bearing the name Mary Watson stood at the head of the grave. The soil had not yet properly settled; the gravestone itself wouldn't be placed for another few months.

'Here you are, my dear,' said Watson gently, 'Violets. I'll bring heliotropes next time. I remember they were your favourite.'

He shifted to give his leg room to stretch – the damned thing still twinged after hard use, and the incident at the Underground station had jarred it. He massaged his aching knee, thinking grumpily of all the wags who had written to tell him where he did and did not have a wound. Some seemed to think that being shot once somehow excluded being shot twice in that terrible killing field.

Watson dug his thumb into the old scar and felt the tight muscle loosen at last. He shifted his position so that the knee wouldn't cramp again. Once settled, he took off his mourning gloves and laid a bare hand over the grave, almost as though he still held Mary's hand in his.

'Well, Mary, it's done. I've written every story that I could about him. I can't say that it's given me peace yet, but perhaps that will come. I'm sorry you couldn't be here for the end, but thank you for being the start of it. It's almost been like being with him again, to write them. And you were right. They serve as a monument to him, since he can't have a grave.'

No body had ever been found, and so Holmes had no burial place. Even Moriarty had washed ashore at a little village days later, but of Holmes there'd been nothing but a bedraggled scarf.

The lack of Holmes's body (Watson could never think the word corpse) made the almost unbearable news very difficult to accept, despite the fact that Watson had seen the killing ground and all the evidence – including Holmes's treasured note – for himself.

The lack was worse even than a burial at sea, Holmes's body cast adrift with no plot of soil, no memorial. It cast a sense of unreality to Watson's loss, and gave his grief no anchor where it could come at last to rest.

His Mary had understood how his grief had cast him adrift. She had suggested he take up his pen again, to make a monument to his dear friend in words if there could not be one of stone.

And so Watson set about writing one. All of the stories, including that awful, final story, would be published each month until the end of this year. The world would finally know what a champion it had lost.

'I miss you both terribly,' Watson said softly, flexing his fingers in the green grass. 'My two great friends.'

He and Mary had been very fond of each other, even if theirs had never been a towering passion.

On the first anniversary of Holmes's death, Watson had returned home drunk, weeping and apologising for not being the husband she deserved.

'Hush, John,' Mary had soothed him, 'You're a good husband. You're kind and gentle and generous. I know we're more friends than lovers, but I'm content. I'm mistress of my own household here, and not a servant in another's. You allow me so much independence, and to run the business of the practice, which I know you hate. It bores you so. I know how much you miss him.'

'You are the very best of women,' he'd told her. But he was the best part of my life.

He often wondered if he'd spoken the latter out loud to her. If so, she'd never admonished him with it. Next day, when he'd recovered, they never spoke of it. He never drank to excess again while she was alive. He couldn't trust himself.

Watson brushed his moustache with his knuckles, to cover the tight pursing of his lips and hide the sudden surge of emotion.

Watson would have mourned Sherlock Holmes as fully and as long as the dear Queen still mourned her consort, but they had been friends, no more. It was unseemly for his grief to be expressed for more than a month. It was unseemly to be so mired in grief at all, and for someone not his wife. For a man, no less. So Watson had worn his dark suit and armband for the month and packed his sorrow away inside himself afterwards. Mary knew, of course – hence her suggestion that he write.

She felt – they both did – that if he could write these stories, Watson could at last let go of his grief. He could let go of Holmes and resume a full life with Mary.

Watson patted the soil under his fingertips. Oh, his good and sweet-natured Mary. Had any man ever been so fortunate in his choice of bride? She'd ever been kind about his attachment to Holmes, never grudging the time he spent chasing outré mysteries of the type that had brought her to their door.

Far from pining at home, Mary had taken up the running of the household and the practice, as though born to manage such affairs. After Switzerland, Watson, never terribly interested in the business side of his practice – and frankly barely interested in the medical side of it, given his years as an army doctor and then at Holmes's side – continued to leave those matters in his wife's capable hands.

Mary had been patient but ever forward-looking. They tried again and again for a child. Each of the miscarriages was devastating.

The last miscarriage, three months ago, had been the most devastating of all. All his medical knowledge and skill had proven useless, just as all his courage and strength had been useless when Holmes had met his end. Their daughter was birthed dead, the cord around her little neck. Mary had bled and bled and bled from the arduous labour and fruitless delivery, and nothing could be done. Mother and daughter died hours apart. Their new beginning had become instead an echo of a bloody battlefield death.

Here in the churchyard, by the grave in which his wife and daughter lay, a grieving thought came to him.

I'm a widower twice over.

The unbidden thought startled him. The words were new, but the feeling was not. Twice bereft, and the account of Holmes's death he had lately written had entwined that loss along with Mary's now.

I'm a widower twice over. Childless, wifeless, friendless.

Watson grimaced. He brushed the loamy soil from his fingers and proceeded to pull the more vulgar growths from the site: dandelions, a tuft of knapweed and a single sprouting thistle.

'I'm not sure what I'll do with myself now,' Watson told the grave as he pulled out the unwanted plants, 'The thought of continuing in general practice appals me. I have much more sympathy now for Holmes's perpetual cry of tedium. Perhaps I should follow Wiggins' lead and try my hand at journalism, though I hear there may be an opportunity to work as a police surgeon. I'm not so sure Scotland Yard will have me. Every corporal, sergeant and detective there thinks Lestrade, Gregson and Jones are based on them. Of course, some of them are right, but I challenge them to accurately identify themselves. Half of them think they inspired Bradstreet, and he's actually real. '

Watson pushed the little vase of flowers more firmly into the earth, taking pleasure in the simple comforts of the scent of soil, violets and other greenery, of bees humming in the flowering rose shrub along a nearby plot while birds called overhead, and of the warm sun on his skin that reminded him of hard yet happy days toiling on his father's gold claim before the scandal struck.

Had he not been so attuned to nature in that moment, Watson might have missed the subtle hiss that sent the hair standing on end up his arms and neck to every follicle in his scalp.

Then he saw it – the sinuous coils of an adder writhing towards him over Mary's grave, dark grey scales marked with a black zig-zag stripe, red eyes unblinking as it slithered towards his bare hand. The reptile – the only venomous snake native to these isles – compacted its great coils as its mouth opened, revealing glistening fangs, and rose up, about to strike.

Watson, too, reared back, snatching up his walking stick as the creature struck and missed. The heavy weight of its body barely fell as it curled and coiled about for a second attack. Watson swung his cane like a cricket bat at the lunging narrow head. If those fangs once connected with his skin, he'd be in for an ugly death.

The thought both chilled him and steeled his resolve.

The stick connected hard with the creature, but Watson was too experienced to be complacent. He swung the cane down and beat the venomous thing on the head once, twice, then a third time to be sure. It lay twitching gruesomely until he took up a stone from the path and beat its head until it was of no further danger.

Watson stood, one fist clasped around the bloodied stone, the other around his cane, his breath coming fast yet steady, his eyes bright, skin flushed. He was surprised to realise he was smiling. Oh, but that reminded him of the old days of adventure! Even though the matter was nothing more sinister than an adder disturbed while sunbaking. He felt more alive, more awake, than he had in years. Since Switzerland.

His smile faded. Mary had been his friend, a good wife and business partner, and he had loved her in that fashion. But she'd never been the one to light the fire in his breast.

He is dead and she is dead and I deserved neither and I'm alone. Again.

Watson flung the lifeless snake and the stone into the shrub, wiped his hand on his handkerchief and left the cemetery, as melancholy as when he had arrived.

He was wholly unprepared for the telegram awaiting him in his lonely Kensington home.

It lay with the early mail on the sideboard. At first, Watson let it be. He wished to wash his hands after so strenuous and sorrowful a morning. A peculiar morning, as well. Providence had clearly chosen to present him, preoccupied as he was with Holmes, with grotesqueries as strange as those that once heralded a tangled and dangerous case.

With clean hands, Watson took up the mail and in the spirit of his strange day, decided to employ Holmes's methods in sorting it. That thin, cheap envelope no doubt harboured a request for donations to worthy causes that Mary had supported. Next was a sturdier envelope, address typewritten, which smacked strongly of a bill that he was in no mood to see. He set these aside and regarded the telegram and the final, thick envelope with a frown.

He ought to open the telegram, but he couldn't imagine it contained good news. Gone were the days when such missives were the harbingers of great adventures.

The envelope was of thick, high quality paper, also typewritten but unlike any official letter he'd ever received from a creditor or a bank. A friend or acquaintance would surely have handwritten the address. In any case, Watson couldn't think of a single acquaintance who'd use such excellent paper.

It might have been mail related to the Strand stories, but those often pedantic missives generally went either to Burleigh Street, or to Baker Street. Mrs Hudson sent them to him every week or so through one of the street boys.

The letter was one more mystery in a day of oddities.

Well, if a mystery was to be combined with bad news, he'd like at least to have some strong drink as recompense. Watson poured a measure of scotch from the decanter, took up the letter opener, and slit open the telegram.

He stared at it for long moments before it fell from his trembling fingers onto the desk.

It read:

Come at once if convenient. If inconvenient, come all the same. – S.H.

Chapter Two

Doctor Watson stared at the telegram, his mouth dry, his heart racing. The initial shock – a surge of joy shrivelling to cinders at the almost instant realisation that it couldn't possibly be from Holmes – gave way to the most incandescent blaze of utter rage.

The first telegram Holmes had sent Watson to summon him from his cosy hearth at his and Mary's new home had read thus. Watson had immediately risen to his feet, startling Mary with his urgency. Once she'd seen the summons, she'd smiled and said that of course he must go.

It became a private joke, that Holmes would send for him with that wording: Come at once if convenient. If inconvenient, come all the same. – S.H. Those words had augured so many exciting and happy times, in cases both wonderful and dreadful.

Watson hadn't written of those telegrams in any of his stories, not even the ones today delivered to the publisher. This little joke he and Holmes had shared was too personal to place in print.

And now someone had dared play such a cruel and hurtful trick as to send him a telegram, as though from Holmes, to summon him to God only knew where. Watson had half a mind to find out so that he could go along and thrash the fellow. Instead, he screwed up the yellow paper and pitched it into the wastebasket by his desk.

Refusing to think more about it, Watson attacked the mysterious letter with the silver-bladed opener. Within were a number of folded, official-looking papers. More puzzled than ever, he drew out the bundle and flattened each upon the desk.

The doctor's quizzical frown deepened. On opening the documents, he found a ticket on the steamship Lenora Ann, in the name of Doctor Ormond Sacker. On closer inspection, the ticket proved to be for a first class berth. The destination: Melbourne, in the colony of Victoria.

Behind this ticket was a letter of introduction, which begged Captain Esmond Deville of the Lenora Ann to provide all aid to Doctor Sacker on his journey and disembarkation. A second letter was addressed to one Mrs Gallagher, proprietress of a guest house on Collins Street in Melbourne, recommending Doctor Sacker as a tenant.

Watson turned the envelope over in his hand, sure that he had read it correctly, and there, yes!, was his own name and address, typewritten upon the outside. Yet all of its contents related to travel documents for this Doctor Sacker.

An immediate suspicion unfurled in Watson's mind. It expanded with several other equally unpalatable surmises. Teeth gritted in anger, Watson retrieved the crumpled telegram from the wastebasket and smoothed it out upon the desk.

The telegram had been sent to him from Palmerston, a port on the north coast of Australia. Hadn't Darwin on his Beagle seen the harbour there? Watson recalled a reported gold strike near the town, the year before he'd enrolled in medical school. He'd wondered at the time whether his father had gone there to try his terrible luck once more.

Memory of his father and therefore of his late brother made Watson scowl and soured his temper further.

Some damned charlatan intended to lure him to the other side of the world by pretending to be Holmes, unaware that Holmes was dead.

Or, said the writerly part of his mind, the over-imaginative part that longed for Holmes's death to be recognised as a terrible mistake, surely to be rectified – or it is Holmes himself, alive, by god. Alive!

The lurch of desperate hope plummeted as swiftly once more into fury. Watson honestly didn't know which prospect made him the more livid. Either instance was a cruel trick, the one perpetrated by some old enemy or new antagonist filled with spite, and the other, oh, the other, perpetrated by his dearest friend, the man he...

Watson bundled up the papers and shoved them haphazardly into his pocket, before drawing on his coat, hat and gloves and storming out of the house, hardly knowing what he'd say when he reached his destination.

His arrived at Baker Street, keeping his temper with some effort so as not to alarm Mrs Hudson or rouse her own rare but intimidating temper. He had first truly witnessed her ire after she'd realised that his stories represented her as a woman much older than her actual years – in her late thirties, when he and Holmes had first resided at Baker Street. 'To protect your privacy,' he'd protested at her sharp irritation.

'You might have named me Mrs Smith, then, and not given the address!'

But that had been in the first book, when Watson had thought to encourage business to their door. Mrs Hudson had forgiven him, eventually, and only because she was entertained by having such venturesome lodgers.

After necessary greetings, however, Watson ran out of patience for niceties.

'You haven't received any letters or parcels of any kind?' he asked, 'You've not been bothered by strangers asking after me?'

'Oh, plenty of those, Doctor Watson,' said Mrs Hudson, her mild Scottish burr intensifying with wry amusement, 'Hardly a day goes by without some impertinent fellow or other wanting to see Mr Holmes or yourself. Some refuse to believe that it's impossible. Last week, one even made it all the way into the house, intruded upon the rooms and began to go through Mr Holmes's papers! I had to chase him out with a broom!' Her tone was filled with hearty satisfaction.

'Last week?'' Watson asked, puzzled, 'But surely 221B does not still contain Holmes's papers.'

'His papers, his pipes, his scientific equipment, his clothes, his music and violin: all of it!'

'But why hasn't his brother come to clear it all away?'

Mrs Hudson's expression softened into kindness. 'Mr Mycroft Holmes says he can't bring himself to do so. He pays the rent and begs that I leave everything as it is until he has the heart for it. It is, I suppose, an easier tenancy to have papers but no Mr Holmes to make his terrible messes, though I confess I miss him. As I know you do.' Mrs Hudson patted Watson's arm. 'It's much too quiet without you both. Even on his own he was too quiet by half. I believe he was lonely, once you married, though he pretended otherwise.'

Oblivious to Watson's troubled reaction to this claim, Mrs Hudson patted his arm again. 'I suppose you must be lonely yourself, now, Doctor. The service for Mrs Watson was very lovely, though, and you spoke so beautifully. If you'd ever like a landlady once more, I'd be so glad to have you back, when Mr Holmes's brother feels he can manage to clear the rooms.'

Watson avoided giving an answer, not knowing how to reconcile the sudden longing to come back to Baker Street with the anguish at the thought of returning alone to the home where he and Holmes had nurtured their friendship.

'I must see Mycroft Holmes.' If Mrs Hudson had no clues for him, then surely the brother, whom Holmes had declared had "art in the blood" to an even greater degree than himself, might.

Watson thought it ominous that Mycroft Holmes maintained his brother's rooms. He wouldn't have believed either of the Holmeses to be so sentimental. Ominous or auspicious. As with many things touching on this shocking matter, he was not sure how to feel. So much depended on the truth behind these bizarre communications.

He made his way in rising agitation to Whitehall and thence to the inconspicuous entrance of the well-appointed but discreet Diogenes Club, close to Queen Anne's Gate. He'd been here once before, to deliver the terrible news of Holmes's loss to his only known relative. At the time Mycroft had seemed unruffled, though kind enough towards Watson's own barely-contained grief.

Too much didn't make sense.

He managed at least to hold his tongue on reaching the Diogenes and being shown into the Strangers' Room, where he pulled off his gloves and hat, thumped them onto the table. He proceeded to march up and down, his stride as martial as if he were off to war.

Mycroft Holmes's bulk filled the doorway. The door itself was not yet closed before Watson bent a blazing eye on him.

'Tell me straight, Mr Holmes. Why do I hear from Mrs Hudson that you're maintaining Holmes's flat?'

Mycroft Holmes did not betray alarm at the sudden exclamation. Instead, he ignored Watson for as long as it took to pour the doctor and himself each a glass of brandy from the cabinet.

'You are much exercised, Doctor Watson.'

'I have had a vexing morning, and it grows more puzzling. I went to Mrs Hudson seeking news on whether some scoundrel had used her to send me a most insolent communication. She told me you are keeping our old rooms intact and untenanted.'

Mycroft Holmes's sad smile halted Watson in his indignation.

'It is so,' said Mycroft Holmes, 'And no-one is more surprised than I, that I find the finalisation of my brother's affairs so difficult. I'm sure that Sherlock would blame it on what he calls my infernal laziness, but the truth is that it's a sad business. He was my last living close relative, and each time I feel that I should tend to the matter, I find that my feet will take me anywhere but Baker Street.'

Watson knew that heartsore condition only too well. He had been to Baker Street but a handful of times since Holmes's death, and only when he had a purpose that couldn't be avoided.

With less violence than he'd initially intended, Watson took the papers from his pocket and presented them to the elder Holmes.

'I received these papers this morning,' he said, allowing Mycroft Holmes to take them from his fingers, 'This telegram uses the very wording with which Holmes once called me to cases at Baker Street. What intolerable scheme is this? Who would find profit in such cruel humour?'

Mycroft perused the papers, one eyebrow raised. 'These are indeed curious and, as you say, unkind. Who do you believe sent them to you?'

'I could not possibly guess.' Watson's mouth and brow were drawn into tight, unhappy lines, for his heart was too troubled and his mind too confused to express the deduction that hovered at the fringe of thought. *Your brother is alive and has sent for me.* The notion was too mad and too cruel for utterance.

The words dried in his mouth, moreover, at the searching look to which Mycroft Holmes subjected him. He had once been used to such looks from Sherlock Holmes, as Holmes examined and calculated and deduced Watson's day from signs and marks upon his skin and clothes, his known habits and principles.

'I observe that you have had a remarkable and unhappy day, Doctor Watson,' said Mycroft.

Watson grit his teeth. When Holmes had played this game with him, there had been a great deal of humour and warmth in the exercise. The same scrutiny from Mycroft Holmes felt much more intrusive. 'I told you as much when I arrived.'

'So you did. You made a final delivery of those most entertaining fictions to The Strand Magazine, I perceive, and paid a visit to your late wife's grave, where you had a most dangerous encounter, but not the sole one of the day. There have been multiple attempts on your life this morning, Doctor.'

'Nonsense,' snapped Watson, 'Only some near misses with unruly traffic and a chance encounter with an adder.'

Mycroft Holmes raised an eyebrow. Watson huffed out a breath designed to anchor him as he unconsciously stood to attention. 'It was, as you say, a very strange day. I returned home to this telegram and that parcel of documents. What am I to make of it, then?'

Mycroft Holmes, not to be rushed, turned the papers over and over in his hand. He even sniffed the thick envelope full of tickets. Watson, aware of how Holmes had once poured over clues in the same manner, couldn't help thinking this was a pantomime of sorts. 'What's the meaning of it?' he demanded impatiently, his voice less commanding and more rough with emotion than he'd intended.

'Calm yourself, Doctor.'

Watson stood quivering with indignation before the portly Holmes. 'How can I be calm? I must know the purpose of this hideous practical joke.'

'But is it a joke, Doctor Watson?'

'It must be. It cannot be from your brother.' Surely he would not have treated me in this cavalier manner.

Mycroft Holmes pulled on his lower lip. 'That is unlikely. However, this name,' he tapped a thick forefinger on the name Ormond Sacker, 'Has very particular antecedents. Pray, take a seat, Doctor Watson. I may be able to enlighten you to some degree, although much remains unclear.'

Watson sat as directed. He took a bracing gulp of the brandy to settle his nerves. Much restored, he sat, alert, waiting for Mycroft Holmes to elucidate matters.

'First of all, I understand you know more of Moriarty and his previous clashes with Sherlock than you have written of. Certainly more than you have ever discussed, except with my brother.'

'Not even with Mary,' Watson assured him, 'At Holmes's urging, to protect her and a number of our clients and cases trammelled up with his schemes. I've recorded their final encounter and its conclusion, as you know, and delivered it today to The Strand Magazine. Beyond that, I have kept silent, as he wished.'

'Sherlock was aware that certain of the Professor's schemes touched upon matters of state. Your manuscript, which you were kind enough to send me, demonstrates that you're aware that in the final action, a number of Moriarty's lieutenants also escaped the net. Her Majesty's finest agents have been operating in the field in the years since Moriarty and my brother's death to stem the last of that tide of crime and treachery. This name here, Ormond Sacker, was an alias last used by one such agent, with whom we lost contact in spring this year, when he was in the Colony of Natal. The reappearance of the Sacker name may infer that the agent was not killed after all, or it may indicate that some other fate befell him and that either a fellow agent or, less likely, an enemy, is using it to enlist your assistance in the ongoing assignments.'

'But why communicate with me, and in this fashion? And why now?'

'The timing may well be coincidental, though I hardly think so, with three separate attempts made on your life this day alone.'

Watson's swallowed the last of the brandy, though in his agitation he spilled a little over his fingers. He mopped up the liquor with his handkerchief – remembering suddenly how he'd employed another earlier to clean his hands from the adder's blood – and he looked beseechingly at Mycroft Holmes.

'Has someone truly been attempting to kill me?'

'So I read it, Doctor Watson. It beggars belief to accept that three close accidents on the day you receive this telegram and the accompanying parcel are unrelated. As to your first question – well, Sherlock's reports to the Government showed that you knew almost as much as he on these cases. Certainly you retain your notes. Perhaps your advice and assistance are vital. If the trail has taken our agent to one of our Australian colonies, where I believe you lived for a time, it must be important.'

'Indeed. If any of Moriarty's black crew remains free, then I'd certainly be prepared to do my utmost to see the end of them. We fought too hard and lost too much to allow these lawbreakers to continue with their criminal activities.'

'It relieves me to hear you say so, Doctor Watson, for I believe you must depart, using these tickets, without delay. I would very much appreciate it if you'd investigate the matter. It may be dangerous, of course. I surmise that Her Majesty's own agent has sent the summons, but I can't be certain. It may be a trap.'

'And it may be a genuine appeal for assistance,' said Watson staunchly.

'Indeed. And the risks of ignoring a true appeal may outweigh the risks of subterfuge. You would at least be forearmed with caution. What do you say, Doctor – will you act on Her Majesty's behalf to help her agent complete my brother's work?'

'I should be glad to render any service I may to Her Majesty.'

'Good man. I shall send a porter to your home to pack for you. You may lodge in my spare room in Pall Mall until the Lenora Ann sets sail on Friday, which is the day after tomorrow.'

'Surely not,' said Watson, thunderstruck, 'You can't mean that I leave London at a moment's notice for the Antipodes? And who is to say that a final attempt on my life – if indeed those incidents today have been assassination attempts – won't be made on the voyage?'

'I believe that to be most unlikely. If you fail to return to your rooms at all today, they can't pick up your trail, except through the Diogenes Club, and as you well know, this is not a club of talkative men.' Mycroft Holmes beamed, pleased with his little joke about his notorious club where speech even among members was forbidden.

'What of my practice? My luggage?'

'The luggage and necessities of travel can easily be obtained, if you'll give me your latchkey. As for your practice – it's easy to see you have been unhappy with the work. If you're amenable, I know of a man seeking a medical practice in your very neighbourhood. If you would allow me to handle so delicate a transaction, I'll see to it that you get a fair price.'

The more cautious part of Doctor Watson knew this to be precipitous and potentially ill-advised. Who was it who summoned him, and so callously with Sherlock Holmes's own words? What ill-famed lieutenant of Moriarty's had slipped the net and was even now conspiring to murder him, to keep him from answering the summons? What contribution had he to make to such a manhunt?

Yet he was heartsore. Now the stories were written, a chasm of lonely days and nights, of listlessness and boredom, opened before him. Grief was still his daily companion. Here instead was the offer of, at the very least, distraction.

He'd sworn never to return to Australia, but he'd been a boy then, flying from scandal and disaster. Now he was middle-aged and once more cut off from family and friend alike. And after all – why not? Whatever the assignment held, whatever the challenges, anything would be better than this slow wasting away from sorrow here in London.

Watson's blood stirred at the old call to action. He would answer it, travel back to the land that had taken so much from him, and if he came upon any confederate of Moriarty's, well then, he'd at last have his vengeance on that gang for murdering his friend.

He might also have a crisp word in season for the agent who had sent him that telegram, too, not least to discover how he'd known of the long-standing and private joke. Watson's anger still simmered from the shock he'd received on opening the telegram. The impersonation of his friend remained a cruel and unnecessary ploy. He'd certainly make his feelings on the subject known.

The deeper and more complicated disappointment – that the message was not from Holmes after all – he would keep to himself.

'I'll do it,' said Doctor Watson firmly, shaking Mycroft Holmes's hand with a steady grip.

Chapter Three

Upon disembarking at Palmerston in the north of Australia early in the month of September, Sherlock Holmes stowed his meagre luggage at an insalubrious hostel for sailors before resuming the hunt. He found his quarry among the drinkers and opium smokers at an even dingier establishment. His enemy was befriending a Chinese miner from the gold diggings. The discussion was of a young fellow Chinaman who had in recent days sought information about passage south.

Holmes lost them in the unlit streets, however, and had to retire for the night. He still limped, though the knife wound was mending well. He had little patience for the injury. It was his own fault for being too slow to avoid it.

The next morning, he picked up the trail only to find it dribbled with blood. That gruesome trail led to a river and an ugly discovery.

The Chinese goldminer's body was mangled, chewed in half by one of the great saltwater crocodiles that frequented this locality. One of the gnarl-backed beasts was lurking, semi-submerged, in the river not a hundred yards away and Holmes knew he must not linger. Those fearsome reptiles were as fast on land as in water. Even at full strength, Holmes would be hard-pressed to outsprint the monster.

A quick examination of the body showed that the miner had died before making a meal for the brute. Other signs evidenced torture. Strips of skin had been sliced neatly from his face, arms and chest, as wide and as long as a shoelace. His expression was a rictus of terror. He appeared to have died of cardiac arrest after biting his own tongue near in half in a fit. Peculiar marks around the entry to his left ear were blurred by water and the tooth marks of some smaller carnivore.

Holmes made note of every salient fact, then backed swiftly away from the shore, alert for the crocodile and any of its lurking kin. As he drew away from the river's overpowering smell of rotting vegetation and dead flesh, Holmes heard a splash, a roar, then a gurgle, and knew that the poor man's remains would be found by no other.

Holmes sought new avenues of enquiry in Palmerston. What he discovered filled him with alarm and despair, but also determination. He'd sacrificed too much to lose this terrible game now.

Two days later, an elderly Chinese man walked stooped over through the docks. He was bent into an inverted hook, from his long, grey, pointed beard, over the curve of his bowed head, shoulders and back and to the spindly length of his legs. He was fast enough on his feet, however, darting through the throng of people and carts at the Port of Darwin, on his urgent mission.

The old Chinaman's sallow face was gaunt and watchful, but he ducked apologetically whenever any fellow bumped into him. Some of the Europeans bumped into him with blundering, uncaring strides and then demanded he apologise. He bowed and moved on. One tried to strike him with the back of a large hand, but he dashed aside, far more nimble than he looked. The churlish dockworker only succeeded in bashing his own hand on the side of a barrel.

Finally, the old man halted and backed into the minimal shade of a pile of crates and luggage. He pressed a sleeve to his face to carefully mop the sweat from his brow without smearing either paint or putty. This disguise was more difficult to manage in the tropical heat than was safe, but his options were limited.

The Port of Darwin docks thronged with sailors, merchants, traders and other human traffic, just as the berths were lined with clippers, barques, schooners and smaller vessels. Trimmed sails rose like liana-strewn and foliage-denuded trees from the decks of wooden sailing ships, iron hulls and the lighter steel vessels, too. Even on the steamships, the bare forest of masts stood tall, retained in case the fuel should run out on a long journey and the captain have to resort to the vagaries of wind and current. The creak of ropes and the slap of water against hulls mingled with the shouts of men and the cries of seabirds, as well as the groan of hemp and croak of metal emitted by the hoists and cranes, the crash and thump of shifting cargoes, and the rattle of carts bringing goods to and from the wharf. From where Holmes lurked, the stench of salt air, old fish, creosote, horse dung, guano and sweat intensified or grew fainter with the humidity and the uncertain breeze.

Sherlock Holmes observed the small cutter bobbing at the wharf and found at last the face he was searching for.

Colonel Sebastian Moran.

Holmes curled his long fingers into fists and pressed them against his thighs. He was itching to do that brute a severe mischief. Were it not for Moran, Watson would not be in danger.

Holmes made himself relax. He watched as Moran secured a berth on the vessel, carrying the scantest of luggage, a single small trunk, a wicker basket and a canvas bag, on board. Moriarty's last lieutenant appeared unconcerned that he might be under observation. Perhaps Moran thought he had lost Holmes on the voyage from Borneo. It had been a near thing; Holmes had been a week behind in his pursuit.

He was always a week behind the man, devil take him, ever since that fortuitous – or rather, deeply unlucky – encounter in the Colony of Natal.

Immediately following the Reichenbach confrontation and his sudden decision to take advantage of its aftermath to disappear, Holmes had secretly liaised with Mycroft, who in turn liaised with international police forces, to finalise the Moriarty business. Then, having chosen to leave London and Watson, he found he desired a break from his old profession, too. Holmes travelled for a year, following whims under numerous personae, sometimes working in laboratories, sometimes on the stage. He spent several months in Tibet before travelling for most of a year through Asia. Africa followed.

In the Colony of Natal, he had by chance seen Sebastian Moran in secret conference with one of the Boers known to be conspiring against the British Government. Holmes had alerted the Queen's local agent, resulting in one agent with a cut throat and Moriarty's chief lieutenant still at large.

Holmes decided to run this quarry to earth, almost on an impulse. His purposeless wanderings had palled. The man who had never thought himself lonely before he lived with Doctor Watson in Baker Street felt the absence of his friend keenly. This last task, a reminder of their old adventures together, was at least something to do.

Holmes had sent the agent's false identity papers to Mycroft, with a salient report. Immediately after, he followed Moran across Africa, then by boat across the sea to India, across the Bay of Bengal and the Andaman Sea, overland to the South China Sea and to Spain's Philippine Islands, and thence to Borneo. Always days or weeks behind, Holmes pursued Moran, glad to have a purpose again at last, though it was a stalemate game at best.

One thing had protected Holmes throughout the pursuit. For all that the general public was unaware of his alleged death – and Watson's return to his literary efforts kept the issue muddy – his fall to oblivion at Reichenbach was, in police and criminal circles, common knowledge. Their immediate acquaintances at Scotland Yard and in the British Government had been informed and word had spread, hurried along by Mycroft's timely whispers in the right ears.

Mycroft had questioned his brother's decision to disappear when fate offered him such an opportunity. He had conveyed to Sherlock the depth of Doctor Watson's mourning, but Holmes was steadfast. The death of Sherlock Holmes would protect Doctor and Mrs Watson from the vengeful attention of any of Moriarty's inner circle that had escaped; and it freed all three of them from a situation that had become untenable. The nature of that situation he had not described, although Mycroft had certainly deduced it.

When he left England, Sherlock Holmes certainly had no intention of ever returning. Were it not for the terrible mistake he'd made in Borneo, he'd doubtless have faded into lonely obscurity.

Holmes cursed the slip that had resulted in his exposure. After being so careful for so long, that wholly unforseen and unexpected encounter at the Pontianak docks had finally alerted Moran to the fact that Sherlock Holmes was not dead. Moran objected to this discovery, and to Holmes's stated intention to see Moran face justice for his crimes – whether by hanging or one-to-one battle – in the strongest terms.

Their encounter was short and brutal, culminating in Moran's escape on board a merchant clipper and Holmes spending three fretful days recovering from a knife wound to his thigh. Furious at his own carelessness, Holmes limped aboard a ship as soon as the injury allowed, to follow Moran south to Australia.

The second ship met with exceedingly inclement weather during the crossing, limping into Palmerston five days behind the clipper. Holmes expected Moran to be long gone, but found instead that the villain was making inquiries about a man recently departed for the great southern city of Melbourne. One of the people he had questioned was the unfortunate miner who had since made a meal for the crocodiles.

My game is hunting some other quarry, Holmes realised. It explained some things, but almost everything remained in darkness. Instead of wasting time in useless self-recrimination for failing to operate at his best – too steeped in melancholy and aimlessness since stealing away from John Watson – he determined to renew his intellectual and physical vigour and put an end to this business. ·

However, in retracing Moran's footsteps in Palmerston after the prospector's murder, Holmes had confirmed his fears via dreadful news that almost made his heart stop.

Moran had sent a telegram to Ronald Adair in London:

The Professor's opponent lives. Collect termination payment from his medical ally, or I'll return to settle all accounts.

The meaning of the threat was unequivocal. Frantic, Holmes had wired Mycroft, using their old code. The missive translated as:

Moran knows. I wire JW today. Despatch him to Melbourne, Victoria under agent's alias. Do not explain anything; that is for me.

Then he sent the old summons to Watson – though it took him a moment to command the courage and harden his heart to the necessity.

Nothing less than the threat to John Watson's life would have made him contact his old friend.

He hadn't been prepared for Mycroft's reply a day later: Package sent to the June widower. Commission accepted.

Holmes sorrowed for John's loss, but even had he known of Mary's death he wouldn't have returned to London, no matter how he longed to go, or to see Watson, or to resume the life they once had together. His conclusions regarding Watson and himself had been logical and inescapable. Mary's death did not change the fundamental fact that London had no future for him that he could bear to live with.

The whole situation was worse, even, than the debacle with Victor, almost twenty years ago.

John Watson would doubtless find himself another wife in due course, provided he lived long enough to find someone to court. At least the telegram and shipboard billet guaranteed him six weeks or more of safety.

When the good doctor arrived in Melbourne, well, that difficulty must be dealt with when the time came. Melbourne was the current destination of Moran's prey, but Moran had been chasing the fellow at least since Borneo. Who knew where the hunt would end? Where the chase would lead them next was not clear, though he'd formed some theories.

Perhaps the entire matter would be dealt with by the time Doctor Watson reached port.

Perhaps Watson would join him for a final adventure (Holmes couldn't help a sharp surge of hope at the idea, which he ruthlessly suppressed) before the doctor returned to his settled life in London, and Holmes went on to... whatever occupied his time.

As Holmes, in the character of the old Chinese man, watched Moran negotiate passage on the cutter, he considered his options. If he could be certain that Moran intended to travel straight to Melbourne, it might be better to travel with the Afghan cameleers overland south to Adelaide, there to take a train east. Unfortunately, he knew too little of Moran's own target. If that mysterious person knew that Moran was on his scent, he might depart on an unpredictable tangent, with Moran in pursuit, and they'd both be lost. The once great gold rush city was by no means guaranteed as a final destination – the crash following the land boom had devastated the city's economy in recent years. Its population was reputedly fleeing destitution in the direction of new gold strikes in Western Australia, or back to their many countries of origin. Whatever business Moran and his prey were involved in, Melbourne was an unlikely final destination.

No. The only thing was to continue trailing Moran while learning what he could of the primary quarry that led this merry chase across the world.

Satisfied that Colonel Moran had made his arrangements, and furthermore didn't know that Holmes was close on his trail, the detective resumed his stoop and retraced his steps. In an alley behind his unsavoury hotel, Holmes shrugged off the disguise, scraping the putty from his eyes, nose and cheeks, to reveal another disguise beneath – that of a dishevelled, inebriated Norwegian sailor, a variant on his previous alias, Sigerson. Slipping into the persona's mannerisms and language was like putting on a second skin, overlain now with slovenliness, despair and surly disappointment to create a new disguised self.

Holmes dismissed the fleeting thought that he'd grown used to being anybody but himself any more; or that he preferred disguises to travelling under his own identity; or that the name Sherlock Holmes had begun to feel as though it were a disguise too. He'd spent so long hiding so much, his own name felt as much a feigned character as anyone else he was these days.

Aging seaman Arvid Nilsen staggered into the hotel, seemingly drunk before lunch. A scrunched up copy of the day's Northern Territory Times and Gazette was in his fist. 'Still no work,' he muttered on the way past the desk to the back stairs, which took him to a tiny, cheap room.

Once there, he scoured the paper for a ship that would take him in the merchant clipper's wake towards Melbourne.

Towards, God willing, John Watson.

Sherlock Holmes felt the pull of hope, and the repulsion of it, too.

Summoning the doctor into this case had been his only option, to keep Watson safe, but Holmes could not imagine a scenario in which this reunion ended well.

https://books2read.com/ ColonialBoy

The She-Wolf of Baker Street

After Sherlock Holmes 'rescues' Audrey Hudson from a kidnapper, she offers him her upstairs flat in exchange for solving the unsolved murder of her family in Edinburgh. Sherlock's being forced to theorise without data, however – he doesn't know his new landlady and her late family are werewolves. There's a lot he doesn't know about his attractive new flatmate, John Watson, too.

Momentum is added to the case as Sherlock's investigations suggest a much bigger mystery is at play, involving a disturbing case on Dartmoor with a Greek interpreter; Sherlock's agoraphobic sister, Myca; Audrey's long-dead love, Ruby Stockton; and the fate of Great Britain's mystic heart.

Will Holmes be able to unravel the mysteries that have haunted Audrey's life? And can Audrey protect her new pack, or is she about to lose those she loves once again to unknown enemies?

The She-Wolf of Baker Street **was short-listed for the 2024 Aurealis Awards.**

Praise for *The She-Wolf of Baker Street*
'Brilliantly executed' ~ Ashleigh Meikle
'A touching and unexpected view of 221B Baker Street through werewolf Mrs Hudson's familiar yet brand new eyes' ~ Wendy C Fries

THE SHE-WOLF OF
BAKER STREET

Narrelle M. Harris

THE HAUNTING OF BAKER STREET

Read on to sample the first three chapters of
The She-Wolf of Baker Street

Extract from *The She-Wolf of Baker Street*

Chapter One

'What the hell are you doing? Are you *cutting* those plants?'
Audrey Hudson thrust her hands behind her back and looked innocent. Ish.

'I would never dream of doing such a thing,' she said as primly as she knew how. She fit the part. Smartly dressed older woman, salt and pepper hair; she looked like someone who baked and knitted and enjoyed a cheeky glass of white in the late afternoon and had a *darling* little herb garden. All of which was technically true.

The young man accusing her of floral vandalism was not appeased. 'What's that behind your back?'

Scissors, a snip of Aconitum lycotonum *and a set of claws when the mood strikes me.*

Audrey opted for stout denial.

'How dare you?' She was already peeling the glove off, inverting it over the stolen leaves to keep them off her skin. She pushed the scissors inside the glove as well, then balled the lot up and tucked it up her sleeve. Incriminating evidence hidden, she, annoyed – officious little sod; it's not like she went around lopping off roses in Kew Gardens – showed her accuser her empty palms, and an unintended flash of her wilder self.

The lad flinched from the sudden sense of *predator*.

'Sorry,' he said. 'Ah. Sorry. My mistake. I'll just. Just.'

And he *just*, as quickly as frightened feet would take him.

Audrey sighed, stifling regret. She wouldn't even be here, if she'd been able to find another source of monkshood in time. The full moon was looming, however, and residential London gardens were less accessible than the Chelsea Physic Garden. Stealing cuttings was bad enough; but worse to be sprung in someone's private garden, especially if their pets went berserk.

The lad didn't even know what she was. People didn't have to know, to cower at the sight of her.

She pushed away the self-pity, dusted her hands clean and transferred the inverted glove and its dangerous contents from sleeve to pocket. She'd have to start carefully cultivating the treacherous monkshood at Baker Street.

She still resisted calling it "home". It was supposed to have been a home, of course, but after three weeks it was just the place she lived. Alone. Again.

The nosy lad whose accusations, to be fair, were spot on, was returning with someone in authority. Audrey felt an oblique sense of shame, even though she'd done things much less civilised than pinch a few leaves.

The head gardener and the lad were angling across the lawn from the café. Audrey could hear the latter telling the former, in worried tones, that a dotty old duck had been mucking about near the poisonous monkshood. She supposed he meant well.

Audrey couldn't really leg it across the medicine garden to the main exit while they watched. Instead, she strode haughtily through the smaller entrance to Swan Walk. Once through the ivy-crowned gate, she turned left beside the high brick wall and loped off, with a slight limp, at a startlingly fast pace. She'd have run faster in her other form, but her other form did not have pockets.

Audrey was walking sedately, her limp barely noticeable, by the time she reached Baker Street. She unlocked the sturdy, steel-reinforced wooden door of the Georgian townhouse, but hesitated on the threshold.

After three weeks, making that first step into the foyer was still an effort. The emptiness of this large house had weight, and the weight resisted her. The silence of it pressed on her ears; the scent of it was dust and neglect and loneliness.

Having said that, it was still better in almost every way than the house in Morningside on that last day. She'd alighted from the train from London to Edinburgh so hopeful, so happy. Yet from streets away, she'd sensed the horror waiting at home. Her taxi had pulled up short at the sight of the useless ambulances and out-of-their-depth police vehicles. She'd run to her pack, her children, heedless of danger, and no-one had been able to restrain her as she plunged inside her home – into hell.

The smell of blood and cordite and the tickling, bitter afterburns of silver and wolfsbane. The killer had known her family's secrets and their every vulnerability. Whoever it was had also butchered her children, post-mortem, to retrieve the silver bullets.

Audrey had lurched outside again, away from the unbearable sight, and been violently ill on a constable's shoes.

Carrying groceries, which she'd bought on the way home, Audrey made herself cross the threshold of 221 Baker Street, into the hall. She consciously ignored the apartment door on the left. That would have been Conal's flat, where he could guard the pack in her absence. She disregarded the staircase leading to the upper floors as well, where twins Travis and Tara had designed their perfect shared space. She was dreadfully aware of the basement apartment beneath her feet. That would have been Siobhan's room, accessible via the tiny back garden.

Not now, it wasn't. After the first week here, Audrey had filled the flagstones in front of the door with trees in planter boxes – a bay tree, a kentia palm, some bamboo, which would grow fast enough to conceal the entrance from a casual glance until the other foliage did the job. Even hidden, it hurt, that empty room.

Despite all her careful planning, she'd left it too late to make their fresh start in London. All that remained was the bitter taste of shame and defeat, and a house that should have been full of anything but silence. Ignoring all these empty spaces took effort that was itself a weight and a presence. Audrey hurried to her own flat, the right-hand one on the ground floor, and slammed the door behind her.

In the kitchen, she washed her hands thoroughly then stored away the shopping – the freshest beef she held aside for tomorrow's full moon. Smaller cuts of beef and the lamb chops went into the freezer. A whole baking chicken and lean bacon for the week went into the fridge. Fruit and vegetables, because even *weres* needed a balanced diet, went into baskets or the crisper.

Then she pulled on a pair of latex gloves and retrieved the monkshood – which she knew better as wolfsbane – from her pocket. She placed the leaves in a small wicker pot. The leaves would dry in a few days, ready to use sparingly, highly diluted, in her personal tea blend. Like many dangerous plants, wolfsbane had medicinal qualities when used appropriately.

It was always possible to use it inappropriately, of course. Maybe if she ever found out who had slaughtered her pack in Edinburgh, she'd stop thinking about that.

Audrey scrubbed her hands again and shoved the wolfsbane-tainted clothes into the washing machine. She changed into a comfortable skirt with pockets for her keys and wallet – handbags would hinder any necessary getaway – and left the house. She was determined to enjoy the sunny afternoon in Regent's Park instead of curling up, metaphorical tail between her legs, stewing in her impotent grief.

She'd been a werewolf all of her adult life and her senses were acute even when she wasn't in her other form. She'd go and smell the roses in Queen Mary's Gardens, and certainly not steal any cuttings from them, because that, as she well knew, was the act of a barbarian.

The lawn through Regent's Park was perfectly pleasant but too tame for Audrey's tastes. Most English parks, with their neat grass and pretty but regimented plots for flowers and shrubberies, had nothing on the rugged beauty of Scotland.

She'd give Regent's Park this, though. It smelled better than a lot of London. No doubt its proximity was why Audrey's very last Alpha, her Ruby, had bought the townhouse: should she have need of a London bolthole. Audrey had forgotten it was part of her inheritance until she'd begun to plan the retreat from Edinburgh. Baker Street was far from the escalating turf wars in the north – London was too tumultuous and over-filled with both humankind and Others for any one pack to claim it – but it had the benefit of nearby gardens. Hampstead Heath was only thirty minutes on the train; an hour on foot if necessary.

The paperwork had finally been ironed out, the renovation completed, and she was returning home with the new keys when bloody events had overtaken them. Another week and they would all have been safe. Another *day*. Perhaps another *hour*.

Audrey shook off that useless train of thought. As a *were*, she had many gifts, but turning back time was none of them.

As the afternoon cooled, Audrey's hip ached. She rubbed at the old scars absently. A sound caught her sensitive ears – a footfall on grass, rather than on the path behind her. Someone was breathing too fast; sweating too. The scent of both wolf and human. Afraid.

Ahead of her was the odd little statue of the helmeted child astride a vulture. The vulture looked fed up rather than threatened. She knew how it felt. She held still and listened.

The footfalls crept behind her, moving away. A soft foot on earth now, followed by a sharp hiss – whoever it was had stepped in a garden bed and promptly been scratched by a rose bush.

'I won't hurt you, you know,' she said softly, knowing that it would carry sufficiently for whoever was trying to sneak away.

'I know who you are.' His voice was tremulous.

'I'm just minding my own business,' Audrey said. 'Smelling the roses. Looking at the weird statues. Have you seen the one of the boy and his frog?'

'I know what you did.'

'I didn't do anything. That's the whole problem.' Audrey turned slowly.

Hunched by the bed of pink roses was a young man, quivering like a whipped puppy, red hair bright against his blanched skin.

'I was warned about you,' he said. 'The Cursed Alpha.'

Audrey blinked. Forty years ago she'd gained that name, along with her gammy hip. Her family had never called her that, but others who hardly knew her used it like a weapon; or a shield.

This poor boy hadn't a clue. A new werewolf, maybe. Turned without consent, perhaps, as she had been. As most of them were. She'd have thought him abandoned to the dictates of his very first moon, except that he knew who she was. He'd been with a pack long enough to learn that.

Audrey hadn't realised anyone in London would know her, but clearly news travelled fast. Probably through smartphones, she thought sourly. Bloody things. In her day, wolves tracked each other the old fashioned way, by word of mouth, not with *apps*. The young ones were responsible for that. Not like vampires, some of them so old they still struggled with the concept of landlines and television. Ridiculous, prideful, pitiful creatures.

Had Siobhan talked about an app? MonsterWatch or NightstalkerGo! or AngryCryptids. She might have been joking. Siobhan had liked teasing Audrey about tech. Poor bairn.

'You should run home to your Alpha,' Audrey said steadily. 'Unless you've no Alpha to run to.' Her heart thudded fast. She'd brought home strays in the past, pardon the expression. Offered a home to the lost ones. She'd built a pack and made herself an Alpha. She'd lost all of them, true, but that house was so empty. She was so lonely.

'His Alpha's here,' growled a new voice. A woman, steel-grey hair, scowl of fire, arrived on the path. She held out an imperious hand and the cub darted to her side. 'He's not for you. He's not packless, and even if he was, he wouldn't need you and your bad luck.'

'I'm only here for the roses,' Audrey said.

The boy's Alpha – den mother, Audrey thought with sudden fondness, which was what Conal had always called her – drew the lad away.

'If I meet you here for the moon, I'll know what to do about it.'

'This prissy little park's no good for the moon run,' Audrey sneered, though it was more for show. She'd rather liked the idea of having her run so close to home. Hampstead it would have to be.

The Alpha jerked her cub by the elbow and they went away. Audrey watched them go.

The episode had robbed the roses of their sweetness. Audrey moped among them for a while, but the rigidly ordered flower beds made her cross. She meandered west, skirting the open air theatre – Shakespeare in the Park had been Travis' joy; she couldn't go without him – and stopped when she reached the boating lake.

A regal white swan began paddling like a steamboat at full throttle to get past her. A duck flying in to land on the water banked suddenly and nearly crashed in the reeds. Audrey sighed. Animals mostly coped fairly well with her, but when the full moon was due, the scent of her rising wolf drove them into panic. Either that or they'd got wind of the whole "cursed Alpha" thing.

And suddenly, her whole body flooded with grief. It hollowed out her legs and her stomach. She couldn't even laugh at her own stupid damned jokes any more. She couldn't walk in the damned park without. Without. Without…

A grey heron high stepped into the shallows on the opposite bank, sensed her presence and took off with a panicked flap of wings and vanished into the trees. Despite herself, she laughed at how gawkily foolish it looked.

Someone stood beside her on the bank, laughing low along with her.

'They're all neck sometimes,' said the man. 'The swans are worse. Like snakes glued onto an exercise ball or something.'

The man's cologne made Audrey's eyes water and she stifled a cough. He grinned at her, bright and friendly.

'You're new around here, aren't you?' he said.

Audrey, eyes and throat still stinging from his overwhelming and expensive smell, said: 'Yes. I moved nearby a few weeks ago.'

'I'm Bert,' he said, holding out a hand.

'Mrs Hudson,' she said, shaking it briefly. The gold ring she wore glinted in the light. *Let him think I have family waiting at home.* His hand was dry; the grip, surprisingly strong.

He nodded gallantly, like withholding your first name from a stranger was fair enough.

'Bert's an old fashioned name,' he said, 'but it's short for something much worse.'

'Really?' She let herself be amused, since he was so intent on being amusing.

'Adelbert,' he said. 'Told you it was awful.'

'German, isn't it?' He had the faintest of accents, softer, however, and more musical than German.

'Austrian,' said Bert. 'It means "shining nobility" I'm told.' His eyes twinkled.

Audrey retrieved a handkerchief from a pocket and coughed delicately into it, but his cologne still tickled her throat. Underneath the smell of something citrusy and spicy with a hint of cedar was the smell of the grass and the trees and the lake; the smell of humans. Nothing supernatural since the *weres* from the rose garden.

Still. Something about him made the hair on the back of her neck prickle. Adelbert of the Shining Nobility reeked of cologne and danger.

Either that or she was paranoid, primed to howl at strong scents by the overwhelming memory of Edinburgh and the subtle whiff of wolfsbane underneath the blood. She repressed that urge thoroughly. It wouldn't do, to have a 65 year old woman howling at the sun in the middle of Regent's Park.

The lake was quiet now. Audrey suspected even the fish and frogs were giving her a wide berth.

'So,' said Adelbert. 'If you like, I can give you some local tips. Cafes, libraries, bakeries, that sort of thing. There's a wonderful Indian place just off Park Road and my favourite bookshop is Daunt's on Marylebone High Street.'

'I do like a good bookshop,' she admitted.

Beyond Adelbert, among the trees, Audrey saw a wiry man with a stylish undercut 'do, the crown gelled backwards over his skull. He watched her with feline-sharp eyes, pounce-ready.

A slight movement further away led her keen eyesight to another man skulking in the shadows. This one was tall, athletic, slender, with untidy black hair and a hawkish nose. His sharp gaze shifted between Bert and the other.

Adelbert. Undercut. Hawknose. All three, hunters.

Audrey smiled faintly. All *four* of them. Who, she wondered, was hunting whom?

'It's been lovely meeting you, Bert,' she said, 'but I should get home.'

'Of course, of course, I didn't mean to hold you up. Perhaps we'll meet in the park another day.'

'Perhaps.' She blinked her stinging eyes, nodded a goodbye and withdrew along the Inner Circle path.

Undercut was following her, by the sound of it. Adelbert held back. Hawknose was, surprisingly, too quiet to hear.

Audrey reached Ulster Terrace, aware of the traffic ahead and the three men ranged somewhere behind. Away from Bert's overwhelming scent, she could gather more subtle clues, but all three were human. Whatever they were up to, they were no threat to her.

A black cab stripped of its insignia was parked in the shade alongside the park. Not liking it, she turned away. She'd cross towards Baker Street via Marylebone Road; that gave her a clear run, if necessary. No need to get claws out in broad daylight; yet her painted nails transformed anyway, polish flaking from them as they changed.

She hadn't needed the moon to shape herself since well before menopause.

The strong cologne had dissipated, but exhaust fumes now interfered, and the noise of traffic and pedestrians on the path meant she couldn't distinguish hunting footfalls from any other.

She strode purposefully to the intersection. In the event she was being hunted, her best option would be to turn again, rather than lead them to the townhouse. If only she knew the neighbourhood better. Perhaps she could lose them in the cluster of buildings coming up on the left, circle back over walls and come up behind them to...

One set of footfalls hastened behind her, and she turned instantly – her brown eyes flashing a supernaturally wolfish tawny, human teeth bared on the verge of becoming sharper – only to immediately receive a face full of aerosol, wielded by the wiry Undercut. Instinct made her gasp.

The sweet odour of disinfectant and the bitter bite of aconite swamped her senses. Wolfsbane. The same smell and taste that had lingered in Edinburgh (beneath the silver and all that blood).

Undercut strode past her as her knees buckled, as though it had nothing to do with him.

Then a pungent cologne hit her. 'Oh,' said the Austrian, filled with satisfaction. 'It works even better than he said it would.'

He stooped to help her up, pretending kindly assistance to his fragile relative, but his grip was too firm. Through her swimming vision, Audrey saw a plain white van drawing up to the kerb. So much for the unmarked black cab. So much for cleverness.

Part of her wanted to give up, to succumb to fate. She was the Cursed Alpha. She had let her pack be murdered.

But this Austrian had used a spray which possibly had been used in Edinburgh. This man was a clue, a link to her family's killer. She wasn't giving up now.

She let her body become an unwieldy dead weight, playing for time. Adelbert's grip never faltered but other hands suddenly took her arm and helped lower her to the grass. She peered at him: the man with the hawklike nose. His grey eyes were full of concern.

Audrey tried to say "help". She sounded like she'd had a stroke.

'Should I call an ambulance?' Hawknose asked Adelbert.

'Nanny's all right,' said Adelbert soothingly. 'I'll call her physician when she's home.'

The van door slid open. The interior looked comfortable and friendly, and not at all like a trap.

Audrey grasped Hawknose's arm, pressed a finger against his wrist and tapped anxiously, hoping to be steady enough. Three fast taps. Three slow taps. Three fast again.

His grey eyes seemed to pierce her through, then his hand folded over hers and a long forefinger tapped a subtle reply. In her fuddled state, the meaning escaped her, beyond the fact he had understood her SOS.

His other hand fumbled as he knelt with her, holding something small between forefinger and thumb.

'You can leave her now,' said Adelbert, the friendliness gone. 'I can look after my own nanny.' His hand under Audrey's arm, he jerked her upright. She bumped against Hawknose's elbow. The thing in his fingers fell to the road with a barely audible ping.

'She really needs an ambulance, I think,' said Hawknose, rising with her, trying to steady her. His concern held an undercurrent of frustration.

'Fuck off,' said Undercut, returning to assist. Adelbert hissed something at him in German, but Undercut's chagrin only lasted long enough for Hawknose to insist on reaching for Audrey again. Undercut swiftly punched him in the face, and Hawknose went down like a log.

Audrey pulled free of Adelbert, but dizziness felled her. She lay on the ground, panting, and underneath the van she saw what Hawknose had dropped. It looked like a little battery.

A wee transmitter. A *bug*, like the spy shows on the telly.

Pretending to attempt to find her feet, she planted her hand over it, palmed it. Then, still struggling up, she placed her hand to her mouth and slipped the little device between her lips. Swallowed it.

Meanwhile, Undercut had taken another vicious swipe at Hawknose, which left him bleeding on the footpath. He then helped Adelbert strap Audrey into a seat inside and slammed the door shut.

Exhausted, trapped, she sagged.Her captors joined the driver in the front, and they drove away, leaving Marylebone and her failed rescuer far behind.

Chapter Two

Ninety minutes later, the van stopped. Undercut opened the van door and pumped more wolfsbane-laced chloroform into Audrey's face. She held her breath for as long as possible, but even werewolves have a breathing reflex. She gasped for air as he released another dose, rendering her giddy and useless again.

Undercut and Adelbert unstrapped her from the car and bound her again straight after. She slumped, feigning greater debility to save her scattered energy.

They brought her into a dark house that smelled of age and wood polish then on down flights of stone stairs. Audrey resisted as much as she could and was rewarded when Undercut scraped an elbow on rough-hewn walls. She longed to bite him for daring this outrage, but she pushed the savage instinct away. She wouldn't get far, impaired as she was, and a short-lived satisfaction now might ruin better chances of escape later.

Besides, she was in no mood for misguided mercy that would merely create another bloody werewolf with poor impulse control. If she took tooth and claw to these bastards, she'd leave neither alive to transform at the next full moon.

Finally, she was bundled into a plain room with plaster walls and dumped on a thin mattress. Undercut loosened the straps around her torso and arms without taking them off. She heard the snick of the door closing behind them again, and the faintest hum of an electronic lock.

Audrey decided not to struggle out of the loose straps; she'd wait for her head to clear. For all the grief that had gnawed at her will to live these last weeks, she very much wanted to find out who had supplied Shining Arsehole Adelbert with this gas designed specifically to incapacitate werewolves, and if they had been behind the slaughter of her family.

For if she could find who had done that to her poor cubs, she would even that score; oh yes she would. Without mercy, misguided or otherwise.

Audrey woke in the morning, curled up on the mattress. She'd finally shucked the straps from her body so that she could sleep in relative comfort. She'd also taken off her walking boots, so that she could shift, unhampered, if need be.

In this basement, she only knew it was morning because her blood knew when the sun was up. Food had been delivered, but her senses remained too fuddled to know if the water and meat were drugged. Salivation had to be hydration enough for the time being.

She examined the sparse room in more detail. A metal toilet and basin stood in one corner, without any privacy screen. The thin foam mattress was new and clean, but she had no bedding otherwise. The bare bulb which was her only light was unrelentingly bright, and beside it hung a small camera that panned whenever she moved, following her. Three of the walls were smooth and beige.

The fourth wall contained the door with the slot for delivering meals. The slot, like the door, was electronically controlled. The door was solid; reinforced with steel, probably. To the left of it was an indentation that might have been a window, except that it was opaque. Her keen eyesight, pressed close, had identified filaments in the glass.

She didn't know the name for it, but she'd seen glass like it in a disconcerting toilet at a very posh restaurant in Manchester, once. Clear until the lock was turned, when a circuit was completed and made the glass opaque. What kind of scatological sadist made a loo wall out of something that would become see-through in a power failure?

As if she didn't already know Adelbert was a pretentious little shit. And probably a scatological sadist.

When she couldn't put it off any longer, Audrey lifted the negligible weight of the mattress and angled it across the toilet and basin so that she could have some privacy for her ablutions. She left the mattress up afterward and sneered at the pervert behind the roving camera.

She was considering whether to put her shoes back on for warmth when the opaque window became suddenly clear, and beyond it stood her captor, smiling smugly.

Rage responded before caution: Audrey snarled and leapt at him. The glass held but she left great scratches down the panels with her claws. Adelbert's smile became positively gleeful.

'You may try to escape, of course,' he said. 'It will be fascinating to capture your efforts on camera. But you won't.'

Audrey contained her fury with effort.

'You are my first live werewolf, but not my first cryptid,' he explained, delighted to have her undivided attention. 'I have an unparalleled spirit museum, so many fascinating things in jars. One or two surviving live specimens. I have a dragon in a neighbouring chamber, which has been impervious to every flame, tooth and claw she has brought to bear upon it.'

Audrey stood in the centre of the room. Fingers grown hairy and taloned were curled ready to rend, mouth full of sharp teeth distended in a snarling snout. He appeared so elated with her monstrous aspect that she forced herself to calmness, to her human form, until at last she stood before him: a barefoot, 65-year-old woman with disarranged grey-streaked hair and brown eyes luminous with wrath.

Adelbert stood closer to the glass to inspect her. 'You are such a beautiful addition to my cryptid collection. I am presently negotiating for a preserved werewolf paw, but truly, it's nothing like having a live specimen. I must send him a thank you card for alerting me to your presence in London.'

'Who?'

'Oh, an acquaintance who knows of my proclivities. He has helped me to find items once belonging to Alistair Crowley, John Dee, even Madame Blavatsky. Many others of course.'

'Nasty little hobbyist,' she said. 'What do they call people like you? An *anorak*.'

He scowled, pride stung. 'I am a *collector*, of many things, some even quite respectable. Nobody could object to the rare porcelain I keep in another of my houses. I have priceless collections of stamps, also of cars, displayed where fellow aficionados may visit without an inkling of my more esoteric interests.'

'Braggart.'

'I do like the looks on their faces, when they see what I have. In fact, I have a particularly delicious brag book where I keep my collection of humans. Beautiful and pure. Well. While I have them, they are.' His oily little smirk repelled her. 'I do mar them a little afterwards. Nobody will ever have them again, the way I had them. Their purity will always remain only mine.'

This shining fart loved the sound of his own voice, Audrey noted. She remained silent and let him witter on.

'My cryptids I never share either. My brag books are for me alone. I have prepared one for you,' he said. He held up a gorgeously bound hardcover notebook, the paper of it heavy and expensive. He displayed the flowing calligraphy of the handwritten title to her.

Audrey Hudson, Werewolf. Held in the Private Collection of Adelbert Gruner.

'See? A record for my very own werewolf.' His proprietorial gaze on her was foul.

'I am not yours.'

He opened the book and held it up for her to see that he had already pasted an image, taken from the surveillance camera, on to the title page. Even in that photograph, she was obviously not the dear old lady she seemed to be. Her grey skirt was wrinkled, her dark blouse with the little blue flowers at the collar dishevelled beyond belief. In the photograph, her walking boots were lined up beside the wall and her bare feet made her look vulnerable, when being unshod was the exact opposite. She was looking at the camera, and any assumed air of helplessness about her was countered by the wildness in her glare.

Adelbert turned the page and began to read.

'Audrey Hudson, born in 1957 to Stewart and June Green in Newton Abbot, Devon. Younger sister to Ingrid. Schooled locally. Won a few trophies for sport. An unremarkable scholastic career.'

'Where did you get this?'

'Birth certificates and school records are easy. I had to pay a little more for what follows. You were bitten by a werewolf in London in 1974, having snuck away to the Big Smoke with friends for a weekend. You were a wild thing, even then, weren't you?'

She'd been a pretty typical teenage girl, in fact. True, she'd lied to her folks about going to Torquay – London was so much more exciting for a post-A-level exam weekend, with its theatres and night clubs. She, Betty and Joyce had enjoyed a giggling afternoon tea at Fortnum and Mason; a thrilling musical at the Garrick. Then they'd gone dancing.

Joe Clarke followed them back to their cheap hotel; had leered and chased her when she ran; had grabbed her and bitten her arm with terrifyingly long teeth while she fought him off with a squirt of perfume to the eyes. He'd run like a coward when Betty and Joyce arrived with the police.

Joe Clarke had irrevocably changed her life and was nothing more exotic than a rapist with a particularly horrific transmittable disease.

A wild thing? Not by choice, but not tame either.

'Soon after, in disgrace, you leave school and little Newton Abbot to live with your pack in Bristol, with your Alpha, Gordon Edwards.'

That day before her first full moon, she'd wandered Dartmoor to settle her restless feet. The moor ponies she loved shied from her and galloped away in alarm. Her little dog Chester had tried to keep her out of the house when she returned to Newton Abbot.

Next morning she'd woken up on Dartmoor beside the carcass of a moor pony, its blood in her teeth and down her tattered dress. She'd had to bathe in a creek before staggering home, her feet bruised and bloody because she had no idea what had become of her shoes. Her parents were beside themselves with worry, after hearing of her assault in London. Ingrid lectured her about protecting her reputation, and Ingrid's by default. Chester was back to his normal self.

Gordon Edwards showed up a week later and explained the nature of her permanent new infection. He had treated her like his property – 'I sired Joe, so that makes you mine too' – but she went with him, terrified by what she might do to the people she loved if she stayed.

'And then in 1980,' Adelbert was still talking, stripping her life bare and yet missing every important point, 'the Edwards pack engages in a turf war with Alpha William Ormstein...'

Not a war she'd wanted, but the two Alphas were determined to prove their ultimate authority and power. A pissing competition with deadly consequences.

'...and in a final battle, the eight members of your pack are defeated...'

Murdered.

'...and William, styling himself the King of Bohemia, leaves you wounded but alive to show his mercy.'

'To tell others what kind of mercy to expect when William Ormstein wants to make an example of you,' she corrected him.

'Quite.'

'I know all of this,' Audrey said stiffly. 'I lived it.'

'And you're wondering how I know?'

'I assume you're a nosy, prying little prig.'

'This is true,' Adelbert said mildly. 'I like to learn things, and I have contacts with many unusual people.'

'Including William Ormstein?'

'I have not yet had that pleasure,' Adelbert confessed sadly. 'I hope, one day.' He returned to his notes. 'Again, I hope to complete the many blank pages of your story with your help. Here, later you are associated with Ruby Stockton, a Lone Wolf, as they say, until she met you. Her fate is unrecorded, though rumour has it she died of poisoning. Were you too wild even for her? Then you too disappear until two decades later, you appear in Edinburgh using the name Hudson, with a little pack of your own.

'Why Edinburgh?' he asked suddenly. 'My recent research shows that Ruby Stockton left monies and London property to you. Why did you spend so long in hiding, only to emerge so far north?'

Audrey crossed her arms and refused to reply.

'My sources believe you were pregnant when Ormstein attacked, yet there's no record of a baby or any children since then. You have a limp, I know. Were the mutilations deliberate, to ensure that you couldn't have...' he huffed an amused laugh. '*Cubs*. Werewolf patois is charmingly trite. I suppose King Bill wanted no descendants of the pack to challenge him for the Bristol territory again. Or was it mere malice?'

Audrey quivered, pale with rage that this creature was pawing through her pain in a tone of mild curiosity.

'Did you kill my family?' she asked in a low growl.

'In Edinburgh? Oh no. Not my doing at all.'

'You know who did.'

'I spoke to people, well, I don't know if they are really *people*, who were part of that. They told me about you.'

'Give me their names.'

'Perhaps another time. Tonight, I shall film as you transform. It shall be history-making. We'll talk again soon.' Adelbert snapped the book shut.

'You can whistle for it,' snarled Audrey.

He laughed, like that was a joke, then toggled the glass to opaque again.

Later that night, more food was inserted through the slot. Her recovered senses detected nothing tainted, so she sipped the water and she ate the raw steak daintily. She was a werewolf, not an animal, and she needed the nourishment.

Audrey's blood sang at the rise of the moon. Normally, she would be somewhere safe by now. Hampstead Heath had been her plan. In Edinburgh, she and Conal would have walked with the others across the causeway at low tide to Cramond Island in the firth of Forth. The incoming tide would cut them off from the mainland overnight, leaving them with 19 acres to run with the moon without people getting in the way. They would take off their clothes and leave them folded somewhere safe in the centre of the island, ready to dress again with the dawn and take the causeway back to Cramond village.

She'd be damned if she'd strip for this ghoul and let him slaver over her old body as it changed. Scarred, drooping and wrinkled with years and experience in its human form, rangy and hairy and grizzled as a wolf, and all the twisted, unnatural shapes in between – every phase belonged only to her, and Adelbert Shining Creep couldn't have any of it without a fight.

Adelbert regarded her with avid curiosity, pencil at the ready over a rough notebook. He obviously meant to write up more polished notes in the official hardcover book later, in a precise copperplate hand to match the title. He glanced at the camera which tracked her movements in the cell, ready to record every step of her transformation.

Audrey had smoothed her clothes and put on her walking boots again. She refused to hide behind the thin mattress she'd propped in front of the facilities.

So far, the little disk of Hawknose's bug hadn't gone through her system, but she didn't know if her system had proven too much for it. Did it still transmit? Had it ever transmitted? Had any signal been able to breach the stone walls of this underground room? She had to act as though no help was coming. It probably wasn't.

'You should disrobe to preserve your clothes,' Adelbert told her helpfully, an armchair expert in lycanthropic change. 'I shan't be fetching you anything new from Baker Street when I move in there. Don't make things harder for yourself.'

So. He planned to steal her home as well. Audrey added it to her short list of Reasons to Hate the Shining Fart.

The moon rose in the unseen sky. Adelbert rolled his pencil between his fingertips then tapped it on a blank page. The surveillance camera filmed his unmoving captive.

Audrey Hudson lifted her chin and glared at him.

Adelbert checked his watch. Frowned. Made a phone call to check the time and frowned again.

Audrey Hudson remained stubbornly human.

'What are you doing?' he demanded.

'Nothing.' But her thin smile was savage.

'Stop it.'

'No.'

'How can you even do this? We have a full moon. You are a werewolf. You have to change.'

'Make me.'

But he stayed beyond the window, confused and enraged and frightened. If he came inside and she changed, she could rip him into pieces. At best, she could bite him and transfer the curse to him. He wanted a captive werewolf, sure, but he didn't want to *be* one.

Audrey's cool smile did much to hide the effort it took, but a careful observer would have seen the perspiration, the lines of strain around her eyes and jaw, the clenching of her soft and hairless hands.

Audrey Hudson was fourteen when she had her first menses. Becoming a werewolf at seventeen had strengthened her monthly ties to the moon, but as the decades passed she fell into a rhythm, not fighting the change nor rushing headlong toward it like the male *weres* often did, but accepting the cycle into her blood and going with – she'd always found the term funny – the flow. Now she was 65 and had been in menopause for over a decade.

In short, she was not the moon's bitch. Not anymore. The moon waxed and waned, but Audrey Hudson was a constant, and stubborn, and she did not consent to give this awful man the gift of her pain.

When her bones ached and she felt the itching under her skin, Audrey closed her eyes and breathed deep, just as Ruby had taught her. She had no wolfsbane-laced tea to assist in the suppression of her cycle, but her captors had dosed her several times. In meditation, she reached for whatever residue remained in her body, and heard Ruby's voice.

You are the mistress of your soul. The wolf is in you but does not own you. You run with the moon when you can. You must run with the moon soon. But tomorrow's moon will be enough. The moon can wait, and so can you. Breathe, Audrey, breathe my darling. Breathe. Be calm. Be still. Let the moon wash through you for now. You are wild and you are free and you are yourself. Breathe.

Audrey was aware of Adelbert shouting at her, but she'd closed her eyes and breathed through the pain and the effort. She fought the pull of the moon not with the savage resistance of muscle and claw, but with the fluid strength of her mind and the memory of her beloved Ruby.

Breathe, my darling.

Who knew how long she could resist the curse of the wolf? But like a wolf, she existed only now: not yesterday, not tomorrow. She would inhale and be herself; exhale and be herself, and tomorrow would see what tomorrow became.

It was not effortless. Sweat pooled in the hollows of her body, at her throat, in her armpits, the small of her back. She trembled, she resisted, not as stone resists, but as the tree bending in the wind, as the water flowing over the rocks.

She hurt. But she did not change.

She felt the moment the moon slipped under the horizon and the sun bloomed over it. The sudden release of pressure. Her body ached, but the fight was done.

And she fell, crumpled like an empty bag, onto the hard floor, and she wept for everyone she'd lost, and for herself, because she didn't have any fight left in her.

She couldn't see the rage twisting Adelbert's face, but she expected he'd come in to make his displeasure known. Her life had been full of men who'd made their displeasure known when she didn't hand them what they wanted on a grateful platter.

The door clicked as it opened. Adelbert's shoes made a sharp sound on the floor as he entered. Audrey tried to gather her limbs under her; readied herself to bite.

And then a wailing house alarm sounded that Audrey thought would shatter her bones.

'You can wait,' snarled the Austrian. He slammed the door shut. She couldn't hear his retreating footsteps over the strident alarm. She covered her ears.

And then.

And then the siren fell silent. The silence was so profound that she couldn't even hear the sub-aural hum of the electrical system keeping the window opaque and the door locked.

She heard footsteps in the hall outside. Limbs still trembling, Audrey removed her hands from her ears and opened her eyes. With brutal effort, she rose snarling to her hands and knees. Her nails grew sharp. She would fight while she could.

The window was clear, though nobody was visible through the pane.

The door opened, and surprise blunted her nails and teeth.

The man with the hawk nose was bruised and his mouth swollen where he'd been beaten by Undercut, but he beamed at her, pulling his split lip and making it bleed afresh.

'There you are! Brave lady. Let's get you out of here!'

Chapter Three

Audrey couldn't help thinking this knight in shining armour would be more impressive if he didn't have blood in his teeth, a black eye and a marked limp. The cheap polyester backpack slung over his battered leather jacket and the blood spotted over his blue trainers didn't instil confidence either. He seemed much younger, paler and more vulnerable than she remembered from the park.

Hawknose's grin widened at her appraisal. 'I let them think it was worse than it was,' he confided.

'You came for me.'

'I have another commission to fulfil, but yes, I thought I'd better get you first. Sherlock Holmes, at your service. Adelbert Gruner hasn't made you sign anything, has he?'

Her lip curled at the memory of the Shining Fart talking about moving into Baker Street. 'I'd have bit him if he'd tried.'

'That's the spirit. Among his many objectionable habits, Gruner's been abducting isolated home owners and coercing their signatures on property deeds. He's occupying several other suddenly empty buildings. Let's hope the real owners are imprisoned rather than dead.'

'Yes,' she replied drily. 'Let's.'

'Ah.' He didn't quite blush but he seemed to know he'd spoken thoughtlessly and changed the subject. 'Marvellous work, pocketing the tracker when I dropped it, like an idiot. Led me all the way down here to you. Where is it now? It's a useful bit of kit if I can get it back.'

'I swallowed it.'

He opened his mouth to speak; glanced at her belly; blinked.

'You can have it back in a day or two, I imagine.'

'No, no, no, that's fine. More where that came from, I'm sure. It's time we were moving, Mrs...Ah. Everyone upstairs should be properly distracted by now, if Shinwell's done his job.'

'It's Audrey.'

Mr Holmes had poked his beaky nose out the door to examine the corridor. 'Hmm?'

'Audrey Hudson.'

'Lovely to meet you, Audrey Hudson. Time to go.' He beckoned with a forefinger and stepped into the corridor.

Audrey followed him but then glanced back, to three other cell doors, all closed. Hers had been closest to the stairs, and therefore logically the first Holmes checked, but there were other prisoners. *I have a dragon in a neighbouring chamber.* Their matching windows clear rather than opaque; perhaps the doors were unlocked, too.

'Have you checked the other rooms?'

Holmes was peering up the stairwell. 'After I disabled the power supply.' He waved towards a fuse box mounted on the wall at the foot of the stairs. The case was open and the wiring eviscerated. 'Seemed the fastest approach to the locks. Nothing alive inside the others.'

Audrey backtracked down the corridor, opening doors. The first two really were empty. In the third, its walls scorched and torn with claw marks, a worn pile of scrap leather appeared to have been thrown into a corner.

A head lifted wearily from the pile at Audrey's intrusion. Red ember eyes stared forlornly from a fine head of black scales glinting gold in the light. Audrey had met only one dragon, a bluff, deep red Welsh fellow, the size and shape of a VW Beetle. This petite dragon, with her delicate fronded snout and claw-tipped wings, was not from Wales. As far as Audrey could tell, this dragon was not even an adult.

'Get out while you can,' said Audrey softly. 'And don't hurt the tall man on the stairs. He came for us.'

The little black dragon didn't waste a moment. In seconds she had unfolded her crumpled body. Wings outstretched, she launched herself over Audrey's head, and flew like a bullet out of the room, down the corridor, over Holmes' head and up the stairs.

Audrey limped achingly after her, to find Holmes gazing up the stairs.

'The giant bat looked dead when I found it, poor creature. Clearly I need to learn more about chiropteran life signs – but later! Places to be, things to steal. Come on.' He jerked his chin towards the eerie silence of the upper floors.

Audrey stumbled up the first step. Her bones felt brittle and every joint ached. She'd never defied the moon so thoroughly before; she wouldn't try again for a while.

The entryway and sitting room upstairs were deserted. Audrey raised her chin, sniffing discreetly, grimacing at the indiscernible odours. Was that smoke? Was that stink of ozone and burned plastic from the fuse box or something else? Somewhere was the smell of varnish and wet wool; something else was redolent of rotting plaster, and was that the musty funk of rats living in the walls? Gruner's wretched cologne was mingled in there too. Overlaying everything was the blood smearing Holmes' face and clothes, his sweat and grubbiness from a night spent, apparently, prowling the grounds outside. She could only be grateful that so few sounds were adding to the overwhelming jumble.

Oh, that didn't make sense. No sounds?

'Where are they?' she asked.

Holmes mistook her confusion for anxiety. 'Don't worry, I won't let him hurt you again, Mrs Hudson.'

She'd never said Mrs, but so many assumed the title because of her age, and her ring – a gold band, true, but with a ruby inset in the centre. Not truly a wedding band, though not, she supposed, truly not. She let it pass. 'It's not me I'm worried about.'

He grinned again. 'Oh, I'm fine. I have a black belt in bartitsu which I'll certainly use if Alec Reidl comes at me this time. I let him get a few good hits in at the park – I wasn't ready for them to realise who I was yesterday, but that's less important now. As for the emptiness of the house – I've organised a friend to create a distraction. Gruner and his cronies ought to be attending to the small explosion at the stables by now.'

'Stables?' Audrey hadn't realised it was so large a house.

'No horses were harmed in the making of this bomb,' Holmes said, 'though the same can't be said for his vintage cars. A shame, but you can't steal evidence from a foul little serial toerag without breaking a few tail lights, hmm? Ah, this looks like the library. Won't be a tick. Stand guard, would you?'

He vanished inside the wood-panelled room, aiming to fulfil that other commission of his. Audrey stood guard. She was trembling all over but daren't sit down in case sudden action was required. Instead, she leaned against a polished display cabinet full of elegant bowls and figurines. Part of that porcelain collection he'd mentioned. Audrey was spitefully inclined to smash it all, but it wasn't the pottery's fault that Adelbert Gruner was a serial toerag.

Then she spotted something ancient and fascinating. A tiny bronze figure of the she-wolf suckling the infants Romulus and Remus. The metal was worn and pitted, but some detail had remained – the wolf's distended teats, the scores on the body to denote her hair, the attitude of her head, jaws open, snarling at the viewer as if to warn them from approaching her adopted cubs.

'Ah, you found my amulet. I'm sure you identify with her.'

Audrey's head shot up at the sound of Adelbert Gruner's voice, and knew how exhausted and muddled she was by not having heard him approach.

'They didn't stay with their wolfmother,' Gruner continued. 'Shepherds raised them in the end. Nobody ever says what became of the wolf.'

He was holding a gun.

'Silver bullets,' he said. 'I had hoped to keep you as a living specimen, but you'll taxidermy just as well.'

'Silver bullets,' she echoed. 'Someone used silver bullets on my family, just as they used the gas on them. And you know who it is.'

'Perhaps.'

Audrey's fingers curled into fists. Her body wanted to change, to grow claws and teeth and hair; she wanted to tear the smile right off his face. But even if she changed now, he'd likely shoot her dead before her claws could sink in. And she needed him alive to learn what he knew. Impasse.

'Shoot me, then. I'll die as I am and you can stuff and mount a 65 year old human woman on the wall and explain *that* to your guests and neighbours.'

The library door opened again and Holmes appeared with a large, elegant journal tucked under one arm. He stilled.

'Come now, Gruner. You aren't going to fire that gun,' he said.

'I don't see why not. Self defence against intruders in the home.' Gruner shrugged elegantly. 'I don't know who you are, Mister Nosy, but I thought Reidl saw to you in the park.'

'As you see, he failed,' said Holmes, spreading his arms, which revealed the journal he'd retrieved.

'How did you–?' Gruner began, furious, and then, 'Ah. That bitch, Winter. She did see where I put it, after all. I should have seen to her more rigorously.'

'You should have let her be,' replied Holmes darkly.

'Give that book to me,' demanded Gruner, hand outstretched. 'Or I'll shoot.'

'Will you though? You're not a murderer. Yet.'

A peculiar silence followed, in which Gruner failed to hide a smirk. Holmes' eyebrows rose. 'Oh. Your first wife. I wondered about that fall in the Alps.'

'A filthy slander,' said Gruner. 'Give me the book. It's no use to you.'

'My client begs to differ. If anything will get his sister to break the engagement, this will.'

Gruner scowled. 'She won't believe you. She loves me.'

'*Au contraire*. It's one thing for Kitty Winter to be rejected as a witness, seen only as a vindictive ex-lover, especially after the way you destroyed her reputation. It's quite another to see your cruelty and depravity detailed in your own handwriting. A person may consent to be the focus of their loved one's obsessions; few would be pleased to find they're just the latest in a long line of abuses. And this—' Holmes flipped open the book at the most recent page, containing a new photograph and a name, '—will be the clincher that she's just part of the ongoing collection. A new target already, Gruner? To work on before or after you marry your current victim?'

Gruner raised the gun. Audrey tensed. A silver bullet would kill a human man as easily as any other kind of ammunition. Even if it meant her own death, she wouldn't let Holmes die. She hardly knew him, but he'd come for her. He'd come to help others. The foolish young pup. The clever lad.

She steeled her aching body for the leap, and almost did herself an injury by aborting at the last minute when a small, curvy spitfire stomped into the room wielding an upraised – and rapidly descending – crowbar. It collected the unsuspecting Gruner on the left shoulder, causing him to pull the trigger with the impact.

The shot went wide and straight through a glass cabinet full of delicate china.

'You utter bastard!' the spitfire shrieked.

'Kitty, no!' shouted someone beyond the sitting room door.

Before Audrey could act, Holmes lunged at Gruner, using the corner of the journal to bruising effect in an upward swing that connected with the soft tissue of Gruner's throat. Holmes followed the swing through to toss the journal to Audrey, shouting 'Catch!' (she caught) and deftly seized the Austrian's armed hand. A twist and Gruner, howling from the triple outrage to his person, was disarmed.

A heavy-set man blundered into the room, reaching for the spitfire. She'd kicked Gruner in the ribs and then found another target for her displeasure.

'No!' cried Gruner, a heart-cry, as though witnessing the slaughter of a beloved child, when Spitfire Kitty crashed the crowbar into a cabinet of china and grinned like a demon at the pretty tinkling sounds it made.

'Shinwell, get her out of here,' barked Holmes.

'It ain't like I'm not trying!' Shinwell replied. Spitfire Kitty had slithered out of his grasp and put the crowbar through what was surely an authentic Georgian Royal Crown Derby tea service.

Gruner scrabbled to the defence of his pottery collection. 'Stop! Stop it, Kitty! That's collection is priceless! Irreplaceable!'

Shinwell managed to wrest the crowbar from Kitty's grip. Kitty gave it up with a fight at first, then all at once. Diverted from immediate destruction, she grinned devilishly at Gruner, her hands on her hips. 'As irreplaceable as your car collection? All that vintage glass and metal smashes up almost as well as your fancy bloody dinnerware. Put that shit on social media, you arse.'

'I'll ruin you,' Gruner snarled at her.

'You did that already,' she said, and spat on him.

'Shinwell,' Holmes said grimly. 'Get Kitty out of here. The police will be on the fire brigade's tail any minute.'

'You burned my cars,' Gruner wailed.

'Yes I did,' said Kitty, not resisting Shinwell's attempts to steer her out of the building. 'Welcome to cancel culture. Prick.'

Audrey clutched the journal to her chest and tried to think. The expression on Holmes' face delivered the far from reassuring conclusion that none of this was in the plan. His eye was on Gruner's gun, which had slid across the room in the scuffle, and he bent to collect it.

Audrey's eye fixed on Gruner. Gruner's eye was wide and frenzied, first on the smashed china, then on the gun in Holmes' hand, and then on the crowbar, which he lunged for.

A supremely unladylike growl rose in Audrey's throat – she felt her larynx morphing, harnessing the unspent energy of the defied transformation – but the sound was drowned by someone else bursting into the room.

She could swear that Holmes rolled his eyes theatrically at the inconvenient chaos of it all.

'How's it taking so long to pop a granny in the skull, Gruner?' the newcomer roared. He screeched to a nearly comical halt to find the granny in question glaring like a feral beast at him. Audrey recognised Undercut at once, and the look she gave him was distinctly un-granny-like. He took an involuntary, stumbling step backwards.

'This is low, even for you, Reidl,' Holmes remarked. 'Demanding money with menaces not thrilling enough anymore?'

Reidl turned and ran. Gruner, who had regained his feet, hurtled outside after him. Audrey followed Holmes on their heels.

The van which had brought her to the mansion was parked on the drive. Reidl made straight for it, Holmes in pursuit. Gruner, crazed with fury about his precious collections, had angled in the opposite direction towards the stables and his vintage cars, above which a plume of black smoke roiled into the sky. Within the building, a black shadow flickered in the shifting firelight. Periodically, a stream of flame belched from its head, combatting the efforts of the fire engine parked on one side of the building. The hoses poured a plume of water over the exterior of the wood and brick stables; two of the fire crew were fetching foam extinguishers to attempt dousing the fuel and cars within.

Through the open stable doors, Audrey could see that, unfortunately, most of the cars were nowhere near the flames, though she was gratified at how many windows, mirrors and lights Spitfire Kitty managed to break before expressing her wrath on the porcelain. The single crew of firefighters would have the fire under control before long.

'My Bugatti!'

Audrey sincerely hoped his Bugatti was a ball of melted rubber, shattered glass and twisted metal.

Gruner darted through the door, too panicked about his Precious to heed the shout of the firefighter trying to stop him. Next thing, the Shining Fart was dancing about an elegant and admittedly beautiful long-bodied car, the crow-bar scored paintwork bubbling on its sleek 1930s chassis. Gruner finally managed to open the hot door and fit himself behind the seat. She hoped he was wriggling because glass from the broken windscreen was embedded in his bum.

A fireman tried to rescue the vile idiot, and Gruner almost ran him down as he got the car going.

He was getting away.

Audrey was having precisely none of that.

She dropped the journal – it was obviously important, but Holmes could fetch it later – and despite her body's protestations, she managed to leap onto the running board of the car as it passed.

Gruner glared at her, enraged and fearful and full of panic, and slapped at her hands to make her let go. When that didn't work, he pressed hard on the accelerator.

Whatever speed it was meant to reach, the Bugatti hadn't taken to the sudden surge of activity after the intense heat. It gained speed, but only sluggishly. Audrey clutched Gruner's arm.

'Who sent you after me?' she demanded 'Who killed my family?'

Gruner wrenched the wheel left and right, slewing the vehicle down the drive in an attempt to shake her off, but she held tight.

'Let go!' he shrieked.

'Tell me!'

The Bugatti was hurtling down the drive when Audrey and Gruner both heard, dead ahead, a gut-churning, hissing, rattling roar, like someone was shaking a tin bucket full of water and red-hot rocks.The incoming dragon made a relentless beeline for the driver of the car, wings spread, red eyes gleaming, teeth bared. From that wide maw, a ball of boiling red and orange started small; grew large.

Gruner slammed on the brakes. Audrey let go of the car and landed relatively softly in the English boxwood hedge lining the drive.

The infuriated dragon unleashed a fireball straight through the empty rectangle of the windscreen frame and onto Gruner's exposed face. Then, with a final guttural shriek, it vanished into the sky.

Audrey ran to the car. She used the hem of her skirt to open the door, pulled Adelbert Gruner out of the smoking ruin of his car.

She bent over the blistering ruin of his face. 'You know who murdered my family,' she said, voice breaking. 'Tell me. *Tell me.*'

His eyes were scorched sightless and his grimace might have been a grin.

'Wh-wh-what's i-in it. F'me?'

'Anything you want,' she promised recklessly. 'Ask and it's yours. You can film me. You can study me, if you want. But tell me.'

'Aaaah,' he sighed. Multiple pairs of feet crunched hurriedly down the drive towards them.

'Please,' she begged.

'Mmmm.'

'Tell me.'

'Mmmmoran. Sssssto...k-k-k. Mmm....'

'What does that mean? What do you mean?'

The reply was a sibilant gurgle, and then arms closed around her shoulders and drew her away. Holmes, handling her gently. 'You can't do anything more for him.'

Or to him, Audrey thought bitterly.

Men in bulky firefighting gear knelt beside the burned man.

'Did you see that?' one murmured. 'Car just burst into flames.'

'Engine must've been cooking,' said another. 'He pushed it too hard.'

'Ambulance is on the way, sir,' said another gently, but Gruner was moaning piteously and well beyond hearing.

'The journal,' Audrey panted, resisting both despair and lethargy. At least one of them should get what they needed out of this awful mess.

'I have it,' Holmes reassured her.

She managed to arch an eyebrow, because his arms were around her and the journal was too big for pockets.

'Down the back of my jeans,' he said. 'The corners prod a bit.'

Audrey clutched at his hands, feeling for the moment very much the enfeebled old lady people kept mistaking her for.

'I want to go home.'

'Any minute now,' Holmes promised her. 'As soon as I've dealt with the police.'

https://books2read.com/SheWolf

More Holmesian books by Narrelle M Harris

The Only One in the World
Edited by Narrelle M Harris

What if Sherlock Holmes was Polish? What if he or John Watson were Indian or Irish or Australian or Japanese? How would their worlds look if one or both was from a completely different background?

In *The Only One in the World,* we asked a baker's dozen of writers to answer these questions, and the marvellous results are adventures in Ancient Egypt, Viking Iceland, and 17th century England; in 19th century Ireland, Germany, and Poland; in South Africa of the 1970s and New Orleans of the 1920s; and in contemporary Australia, USA, Russia, India and Portugal.

Praise for *The Only One in the World*

'In many ways these are tales about the human condition...even though their ostensible focus may be a crime and its detection' ~ Arts Hub

'Smart, entertaining, and fresh' ~ The Weekend Australian

'The stories are exciting and fresh, breathing new life into a beloved character' ~ Ashleigh Meikle

'Cool...cool...cool' and 'Cool!" ~ Phil Brown, Courier Mail

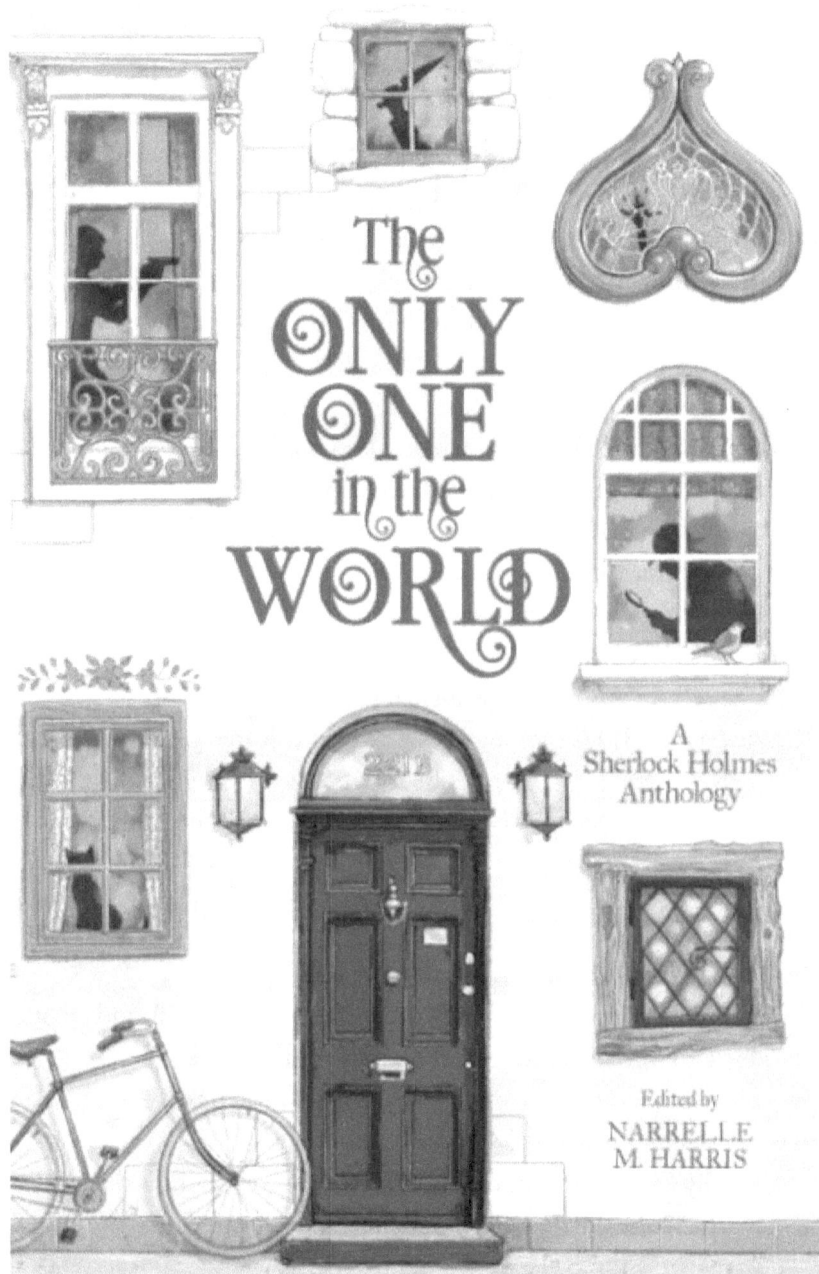

The
ONLY
ONE
in the
WORLD

A Sherlock Holmes
Anthology

Edited by
NARRELLE
M. HARRIS

Sherlock is a Girl's Name

Edited by Narrelle M. Harris and Atlin Merrick

What would the Great Detective be like if Sherlock Holmes was a woman?

That's the question answered in Sherlock is a Girls' Name, an anthology imagining Sherlock Holmes as female, in tall tales that follow the great detective across time and even space.

The stories in this collection, selected by long-time Sherlockian editors Narrelle M. Harris and Atlin Merrick, imagine Holmes in deep space, 1990s Russia, Victorian London, contemporary USA, worlds of magic and more.

Holmes' many Watsons include ghosts, robots, a young boy who doesn't speak, a teenage tuba player, a stranger on a plane – and that's just to start. In each story Holmes and her Watson do what they do best: solve crimes and have adventures!

Anthology authors include:

Tansy Rayner Roberts, Eugen Bacon, Sarah Tollok, Verity Burns, Dannye Chase,

Kenzie Lappin, JD Cadmon, Stacy Lawhorne, Karen J. Carlisle, Katya de Becerra,

Millie Billingsworth, Narrelle M. Harris, and Atlin Merrick.

Praise for *Sherlock is a Girl's Name*

"This collection is a delight. Make some tea, snuggle in, and go on a journey with Sherlock Holmes" ~ Sarah Tollok

"I loved reading the stories in this collection so much – I just want to wrap them up in a hug!" ~ Jennifer Bradshaw

"I really enjoyed this book. In fact my only complaint is that one of my favorite stories is too short!" ~ ReneCat

"An entirely fun collection" ~ Julie

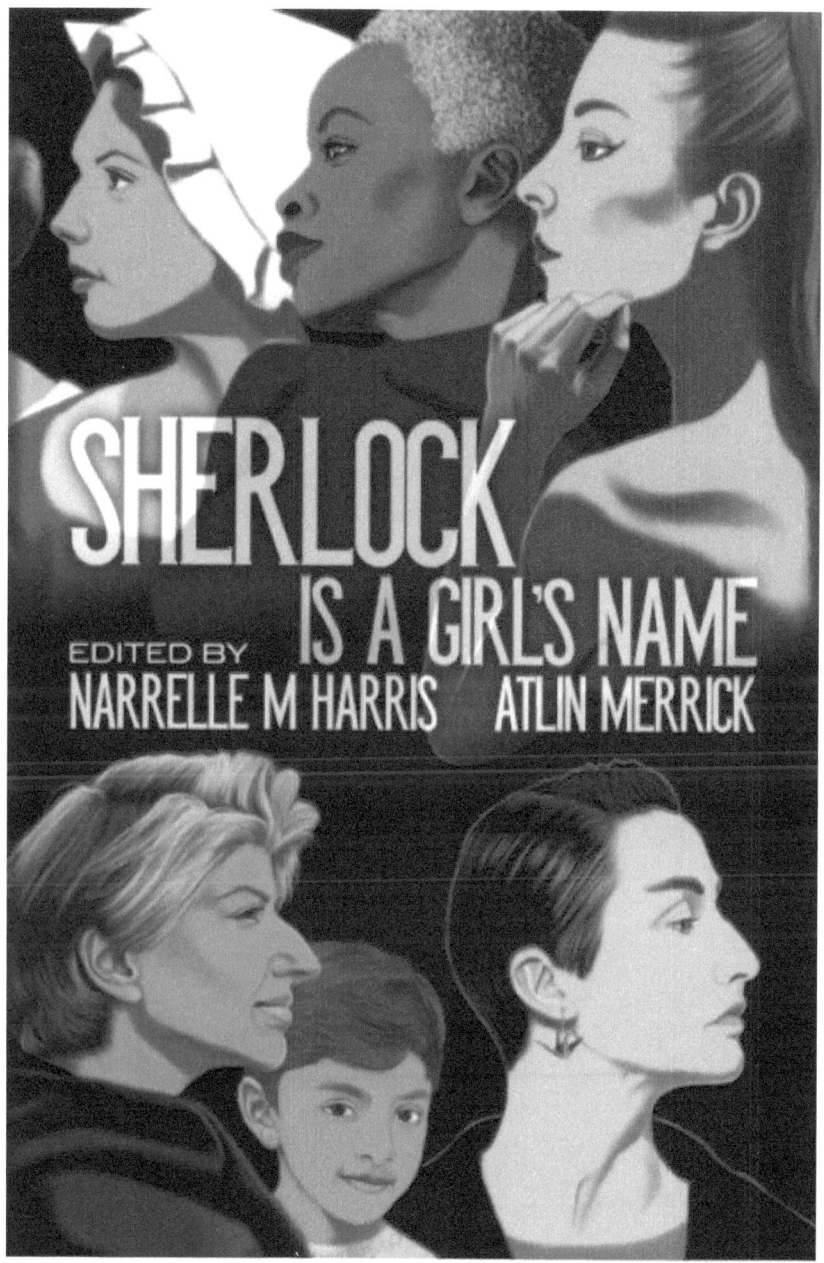

A Dream to Build a Kiss On

John Watson, invalided army doctor and sometimes artist, and Sherlock Holmes, consulting detective, become flatmates and friends in contemporary London.

Love grows too, despite past betrayals and present dangers—for where you have Holmes and Watson, there too are Moriarty and Moran.

A Dream to Build a Kiss On, written by Narrelle M. Harris and illustrated by Caroline Jennings, explores love and family, trust and betrayal, brothers and brothers-in-arms, forgiveness and revenge, in an ongoing tale told 221 words at a time.

Praise for *A Dream to Build a Kiss On*

'Exquisite in detail and structure...'

~ Angela Kam White[1]

'A swashbuckling adventure with more twists and turns than a rabbit's warren'

~ Rohase Piercy[2]

'Caroline Jennings [illustrations]...are an absolute delight' K. Caine, Goodreads

---

1.   https://www.goodreads.com/review/show/2456426643

2.   https://www.goodreads.com/review/show/2614079910?book_show_action=true

Don't miss out!

Visit the website below and you can sign up to receive emails whenever Narrelle M. Harris publishes a new book. There's no charge and no obligation.

https://books2read.com/r/B-A-RKTUB-QFESD

BOOKS 2 READ

Connecting independent readers to independent writers.

About the Author

about narrelle

Read more at narrellemharris.iwriter.com.au.